GOD'S INSTANT

Rodeo, Revenge, and Redemption

BRUCE BLIZARD

Design and Interior formatting services provided by:

SWEETSPIRE LITERATURE
— MANAGEMENT —

TABLE OF CONTENTS

GOD'S INSTANT...

"Been a strange of a couple a days. That's all I got to say," Grady said.

Adah appeared not to hear. "Maybe it ain't that God's so big," she said. "The scientists, they say no matter how close they look or how hard they figure, they can't quite get back to that time when it all began. There's just an instant, a tiny, little speck a' time they can't see through. And the closer they look, the narrower that speck gets, but it don't go away. Maybe that's where God's been all this time. Time and space don't mean nothin' in heaven anyway. If eternity down here is an instant in God's mind, then why can't that tiny, little speck of time the scientists can't see through, that instant, be eternity to God?"

"I don't think about things like that much."

"No, son, I don't expect you do. But this here world wasn't made as a joke, or for anyone's amusement. God was deadly serious when he made the heaven and the earth. Yes sir, it's a puzzle, but those scientists ain't never going to get to the bottom of it. God understands, and we will too, but not while we're here in it, not for our own tiny little speck a time. That'll all come later."

DEDICATION

I've had the good fortune to have five generations of remarkable women in my life: Jesse Shelton, Berniece Allen, Juanda Faye Blizard, Tina Blizard, Jennifer Blizard, and Emily Blizard.

Acknowledgments

First, thanks to my wife Tina for her patience and understanding. This project would not have been completed without the contribution of three talented professionals. Jennifer Ciotta of PencyX Pages (http://penceyxpages.com/) edited the manuscript and insisted on a number of changes to the plot that greatly enhanced the story. I am extremely grateful for Jennifer's insight and for her insistence that I write the best book possible. Romance author Stephannie Beman (http://stephanniebeman. com/portfolio/) designed the cover and guided me through the publishing process. Jim Deatherage was my colleague at Richland High School for 21 years and is the best English teacher on the planet. His fourth book, The Right Kind of Boy, will be released soon.

GOD'S
INSTANT

PROLOGUE

Old rodeo hands say you can tell whether or not a boy will grow up to be a bull rider by the look in his eyes after his first ride. If he can contain the dark fear that is the bull rider's necessary companion, if he can leave the terror buried in a safe place behind his eyes, the boy will most likely ride again. If he can't, and the fear rises to the surface as he sprints wide eyed and open mouthed toward the arena fence, his first bull will usually be his last.

But one young cowboy had managed to bury the fear so deep and hold it down for so long, he was no longer aware the fear was there. For that reason, he was in mortal danger every time he climbed into the chute.

***

Most of the southern half of eastern Washington State was eternally brown. Sage brush and prairie grass gave the rolling hills the same bland quality young people ascribe to the very old. At first cattle thrived on the land and then wheat and apples, and now grapes. From the crest of Rattlesnake Ridge or the Horse Heaven Hills, the reactors of the Hanford Nuclear Reservation were visible. Hanford, known as "The Site" to local people, was once a nuclear weapons factory. It has remained one of the most technologically advanced and dangerously polluted places on earth for years.

A young man stared at the ancient landscape through a grimy window of a small house. In the distance behind Rattlesnake Ridge, he could see a sinister column of steam rising from the cooling towers at Hanford. He squinted against the pale light reflected off the Yakima River and onto the face of his sleeping son. When the child turned onto his back, away from the light, his father bent down and kissed him on the forehead.

The boy's father had risen early to pack his old pickup with the gear necessary for another rodeo journey. When he went outside to start his truck, the rattle of the diesel engine woke his young wife. She pulled on a pair of old jeans and shuffled into the kitchen to say goodbye to her husband.

"Do you want breakfast?"

"No, don't bother. A little hunger will keep me alert."

"How long this time?"

"Four or five weeks if I'm winnin' any cash. I'll send money when I can."

"You always do."

She kissed him on the lips.

"I worry, you know."

"I'm still young. I heal up fast."

"If you break something, you'll have to come home."

"You'd like that."

She smiled. "I love you."

"Take care of the boy."

"We need you."

"I'll be home when I'm done."

He put his arms around his wife. After a moment he nudged her away and walked out the back door. He climbed into the warm cab of his truck and rolled down the driver's side window and took a deep breath of the cool air.

The young woman stood over the sleeping boy and watched the truck turn left onto the two-lane blacktop and disappear. She didn't know he would not return, not for a long time.

CHAPTER 1

Grady grasped the heavy steel bar that braced the two ends of the chute, bent his knees, and settled back into a deep stretch. He stared into the chute at the broad, round back of a two-thousand-pound bucking bull, whose obscene hump rose and fell with each angry breath.

Suddenly, Grady felt very cold. He raised his eyes for a few seconds and stared at the hard blue sky above the grandstand.

"Okay?"

"Yeah. I'm ready."

Grady stepped down into the chute. His world contracted, squeezed by a familiar, primal fear. For an instant his guts churned with the certain knowledge he might be seriously injured and with the tacit understanding he might even die. Beneath the bull's broad back was nothing but an eternal drop into the abyss. He pushed the fear away and straddled the bull. He sat down carefully, feeling the muscles of the animal's back bunch up. The bull was preparing to launch him out of the abyss toward the timeless blue sky. He got a good grip, took an extra wrap on the heavy bull rope, and pulled himself up as far as he could toward the bull's hump with his gloved right hand. He pressed his white hat farther down on his head, dropped his chin, and nodded.

The chute gate opened, and the bull leaped sideways, bucking and twisting to the left. Grady thought he'd lost his hold on the first jump, but his grip held when the bull changed direction and began to spin to the right. He squeezed hard with the young muscles in his thighs. The fear in his guts abated again, and he stayed on.

CHAPTER 2

Grady Cross was eighteen years old and had never graduated high school. He perched on the curb in front of a truck stop near the freeway in the college cow town of Ellensburg, Washington. He was waiting for someone to offer him a ride south. He'd come within a second of winning a check at the Ellensburg Bull-O-Rama earlier in the day. But a hard rain, unseasonable for early September, fell steadily before he got on the last bull of the afternoon. He lost his grip when the big, gray monster twisted to the left instead of to the right as Grady had expected.

He was airborne when he heard the eight-second buzzer go off. He raised his head after splashing down in the soggy arena and saw the bull pawing the muddy ground about ten feet away. He rolled to the left and stumbled to his feet as a bullfighter raced in front of the heaving animal. Grady saw the bullfighter's painted face as he darted between Grady and the bull. The bullfighter planted his left hand in the center of the charging bull's forehead and vaulted past Grady. The enraged animal's lethal head followed the bullfighter. The crowd cheered, and he remembered thinking if he'd lasted just one more second, the cheers would have been for him and not for the bullfighter who had saved him from being gored, or much worse. Maybe he'd do better when he returned to Ellensburg for the big rodeo at the end of the month.

Grady was tall for a bull rider, nearly six feet, but he had the look otherwise. Big hands with sinewy fingers and strong shoulders that triangled up from his waist. His legs were longer than they needed to be, but he was sturdy, and the muscles of his thick thighs strained the fabric of his fading Wranglers. His leather belt was decorated with a dozen silver stars and was held together by a tarnished buckle. The belt was no fashion statement, though. Without the belt, his Wranglers would slide off his narrow hips. Except for the tightness in his thighs, all of Grady's clothes seemed too big.

The rain had stopped, and the late afternoon sun was shining. The mud on his shirt and jeans had dried and mostly dusted off, but he was still sore, tired, and lonely. He needed to get home for a few days. In a couple of weeks, he'd try to catch a ride to the Pendleton Round-up. He wore a long duster, a canvas raincoat split partway up in the back. It had kept the rain off, and he was happy to have the setting sun to warm the soreness out of his shoulders and arms and dry most of the dampness out of his boots.

At last, an old man offered him a ride in a sagging, rusted flatbed loaded with hay. The truck had a big dent in the left front fender. The old man had filled the truck with gas and was checking his load, making sure the tarp that covered four tons of neatly stacked hay was secure. Then he noticed Grady. He moved stiffly and without grace, but with purpose. This meeting with Grady was no accident.

"Need a ride south?"

"Yes sir, I do," Grady said, rising quickly to his feet. He straightened his duster and gathered up a canvas riggin' bag that contained his bull rope, thick leather chaps, and riding gloves.

"Well, hop in. I'll be right back."

Grady removed his long duster and hefted it and his riggin' bag into the backseat of the truck. Then he leaned against the front fender while the old man finished checking the tarp and paid for his gas.

"How far ya goin'?" the old man asked when he returned to the truck. He knew the answer.

"I'm headed home to Richland. I've been rodeoin'."

"You don't have a horse, and not much riggin', and you're pretty well covered with dirt, so I'll say you musta been tryin' to ride a bull."

"Ah, yes sir. I guess it shows." Grady noticed the old man had coarse white hair sticking out from under a rumpled cowboy hat. He also had a deep scar on his left cheek, and he looked vaguely familiar.

"I ride bulls, broncs sometimes, when I can manage entry fees for both and can borrow a bronc saddle. Almost won some money today. Sucker zigged, though, and I zagged about ten feet in the air."

Even though he already knew much of the young bull rider's story, the old man let Grady talk. He listened and said nothing. When Grady was done, the old man turned away and stared off to the south long enough to make Grady feel uneasy. Then, just as Grady was having second thoughts about accepting the man's offer of a ride, a smile creased the old man's weathered face.

"So, you're the boy that got dumped so hard there at the end?" the old man asked. "I know an ol' boy workin' the pens. I was back there when you loaded up. That was a tough bull. I didn't think you'd get out of the chute. You did alright with that bull, son."

Grady was confused, but he appreciated the compliment. Still, the first thing he'd learned about the rodeo was that staying on for seven seconds and getting bucked off on the first jump looked the same to the woman at the pay window.

"Tough way to make a living but might as well do it while you're young enough to survive," the old man said. "It gets hard later on."

The old man's eyes were dark and set deep. His mouth had the stiff set of someone used to things being hard. His knuckles were scarred. Grady sensed he wasn't talking about riding bulls.

"I appreciate the ride," Grady said. "How far you goin'?"

"I can take you as far as Benton City. I got a place a little north and west of there. 'Bout a thousand acres. A few dozen cows. Some horses. No neighbors for a good long ways."

"That'll be fine. I can call my mom, and she'll come out from Richland and get me." *A few nights in my old room sleeping in my own bed would not be bad at all*, Grady thought.

"I don't mind the company."

A thin cloud of white smoke and the oily odor of diesel exhaust briefly filled the cab. It dissipated when the old man put the truck in gear. Grady climbed in, and the old man pulled onto the main roadway.

"My name's Grady." He extended his hand, but the old man did not take it.

"Yeah Grady, I reckon I know who you are." He held tight onto the steering wheel and stared straight ahead as they left the gas station. He pulled onto the interstate and headed south. Grady turned away and sat back in the hard seat. He fidgeted, unable to get comfortable. He was used to rodeo people knowing who he was, or rather knowing who his father was and what he had done.

"I don't guess you got to take me along if you don't want to," Grady said.

The old man ignored him. "I'm John. Hope you're not in a rush. This old rig'll get us there, but we ain't goin' to hurry. You just relax, and I'll get you home by and by."

John's name and his face began to form an indistinct image in Grady's memory, but he was too tired to say any more. He settled back into the seat and stared at the withered landscape rising in front of him. Sagebrush, prairie grass, large rocks here and there. The highway climbed south away from Ellensburg up the first of three tough grades to the top of Manastash Ridge. Grady always made it a point to look back here to see the long, broad, green checkerboard that was the Kittitas Valley. The lights of Ellensburg would be visible in the twilight. The valley drifted west and then curved suddenly northward toward the Cascade Mountains, which were already changing from deep green to black in the shadows of the approaching night. This time when Grady turned to look, the load of hay in the flatbed blocked his view. So, he missed seeing the landscape, but he did enjoy the faint odor of newly cut alfalfa.

"I wish I could sleep, but it's hard right after a rodeo," Grady said. "I'm plenty sore and tired. Ever rodeo yourself?"

"Nope. My boys did. Oldest's a pretty good roper too. Never made much of it, though. It's hard when you need make a livin' to rodeo at the same time. The youngest did it all at one time or another. Rough stock at first, bareback, saddle bronc, bulls now and then. Scared his mother to death. She was happy he gave it up and took to calf roping. He won some money ropin' calves."

"What do your boys do now?"

"Oldest doctors cows in a feed lot or works for farmers and ranchers around home once in a while. The middle boy, he lives somewhere down around Boise with his wife some a' the time. Don't know what he does the rest a' the time. He don't bother to get up this way too much. Youngest is dead."

"Dead?" Grady wanted to ask how John's son had died, but he was suddenly very sure he knew. The indistinct image in his memory coalesced into a name and a face that made his heart race. He didn't say anything.

"Yeah. I reckon he was about your age when it happened."

Grady sat up and turned toward the old man. "You're John Carpenter."

The old man continued to stare straight ahead. The dark was nearly complete, and the landscape rolled past in shades of green sage and brown sand that faded to black as night settled. The sky was the deep blue people in town never see, almost black but with a suggestion of color that would remain until long after the moon and the stars came out. In the desert, it would not be fully dark until just before the sun came up.

"I am," John answered.

He was silent for a long time.

"But it don't make no difference."

Grady turned away and focused his attention on the steep landscape darkening in the twilight. They passed through several miles of dark prairie before John spoke again.

"Look, son, I know who you are. Fact is I knew it when I picked you up. And you know who I am. Won't do neither of us no good to say it out loud. Just sit back and get some rest. What's done can't be changed. And that's the end of it."

"I won't blame you if you leave me off down the road here. I 'spect I can get another ride."

"No need. Don't say no more. I'm happy to help you out."

CHAPTER 3

Jill Marion was only fourteen when the accident that killed her father and nearly ended her own life left her mother an emotional invalid. When she walked home from school every day, now three years later, she had no sense of going home, only of going away. On this day, it was raining when she left school. But twenty minutes later, when she arrived at the house she shared with her mother, the rain had stopped.

Jill lived on a shady street in Richland, Washington. But today the trees that normally provided slight relief from the searing summer sun dripped and drooped in the wake of three days of unending rain.

She did not take her oversized hood down after she walked through the front door. The house was not tightly constructed. A faint musty odor that reminded her of an old woman's house replaced the normal, summertime dustiness.

Her mother was asleep on the couch, so Jill covered her with a heavy afghan and kissed her on the forehead. She sat in a big armchair that faced the front window and watched the trees drip and the afternoon shadows change as dusk settled. She laid her head back against the chair and decided that there was no point in staying any longer. She would leave tonight.

***

In this particular strip of the extreme northwest corner of the US almost everyone, including Jill's mother and dead father, came to the desert from somewhere else.

The rain of recent days was a welcome change from the normal cycle of alternating hot and cold dry spells. The land had once been good for cattle and little else, then the college farmers at Washington State University taught the ranchers to irrigate the land, and the cows grudgingly gave way to apple and cherry orchards. The farmers and ranchers alternately prospered or struggled, thriving in the good years and either starving or selling out in lean times. Finally, opportunists from elsewhere gradually discovered that grapes provide more money and less uncertainty. So, vineyards surrounding ornate wineries began to creep up the sandy, treeless hillsides and crowd the tiny towns. The land was dry and dusty—barren except where the dams on the Columbia and the Snake rivers and the endless miles of narrow irrigation canals brought water.

Even where the land was irrigated, a lot of the ground here wasn't good for much of anything but cows. Long ago, and occasionally even now, scattered herds spotted the dry hillsides. They foraged for grass and held their own, waiting for a date with the feedlot and the slaughterhouse. Then one day, when the rest of the country was slugging its way through the dark middle years of World War II, the US Army came and found a darker purpose for a dusty crescent tucked into a slow bend in the Columbia. The government decided in 1943 that this land of few people, sparse crops, scant prosperity, and three rivers was the perfect place to build a huge nuclear bomb factory. The tiny burg of Richland—once situated precisely where the Yakima slides across a muddy delta into the Columbia—became a boom town. And the resulting nuclear roar had never been silenced.

Locals called the Hanford Nuclear Reservation "The Site." It sprang fully formed from the desert and from the mind of a determined and single-minded Army General named Leslie Groves. The chemical remnants of the necessary horrors created in secret there continued to haunt the region. The nuclear nightmare of Hiroshima and Nagasaki, the mad logic of deterrent strategies during the Cold War, and the legacy of poison, which exploded downward and seeped toward the Columbia River at the dawn of the present century, all had their genesis when General Groves discovered the parched land was good for death too. The people who had long before settled in the desert were at first bewildered by the change wartime necessity brought to their home, but they generally embraced the prosperity that came with the Hanford Nuclear Reservation and mostly moved quietly out of the way. In their place, a scattered tribe of scientists, engineers, and technicians, that would eventually include Jill's father, assembled and put down shallow roots.

People in the inland northwest never developed the habit of dissimulation, even after the scientists arrived, because the people here didn't have time to invent tall tales. Wrenching a living out of the sand and rock was so difficult that embellishment had not seemed necessary. The culture of science brought to the desert by General Groves resisted exaggeration. The region had a dualistic mythology: the scientific hubris that came from a new age belief in the power of technology and the glory of the reactors, and an old-timey faith in the resilience of the land and in the cleansing power of the endless wind and the great rivers.

At the heart of this mythology was the Columbia River. Once swift and cold, but now deep and no longer wild, the river had been calmed, like much of the countryside. But there remained just beneath the surface an uncertainty bred in the union of an ancient land and a mysterious future.

✳✳✳

Jill had lived here all her life, so she was not interested in either tall tales or nuclear realities. Generally, it was people who lived elsewhere who concerned themselves with life in the shadow of the Hanford reactors. At seventeen, Jill had enough to do. She lived with the loss of both parents, one dead and one in a daze.

"We'll have to help each other now," Her mother told her while Jill lay in a hospital bed on the day of her husband's funeral. "We only have each other now." The memory of those words at first made Jill sad, then angry, and finally, resigned. After her father died and her mother had all but removed herself from Jill's world, the girl became silent.

Jill sat in a large chair until long after the sun had set, and the room had grown dark. Outside light rain pattered against the windows. She had not taken off the long wool coat she wore to school every day, regardless of the weather. She pushed back the oversized hood. It draped over the back of the chair to reveal a wet tangle of brown hair. At school, she wore the coat buttoned nearly to her chin with the hood pulled safely down so it was difficult to see her eyes.

Once she had made up her mind to leave, she pulled the hood back over her head and down so her eyes became invisible again. Her mother remained asleep on the couch. She had not moved. Jill left the house and went out into the rain, into the dark.

She followed a route she knew well. She walked six blocks north, cut through a wooded area next to the middle school, sloshed across the school's broad expanse of green playfield, and headed east toward the river. The Columbia at Richland was flat, deep, and slow. During the hot and sunny summer months, the calm channel was busy with jet skis and power boats. On shore oily teenagers preened for each other, while wary young mothers guarded toddlers who splashed in the shallow water. But on this rainy autumn evening, the river and the long green line of Howard Amon Park were both deserted. The rain made the surface of the river seem alive with countless tiny ripples, perfect watery circles that expanded then disappeared as they moved away to the south with the slow current.

She was familiar with both the river and the park. She had spent many hours there in the three years since the accident, usually at night and always alone. She had been asleep in her father's car when it flipped on the freeway in the middle of the night. But when she woke up in a hospital bed after three days, her only memory was of her mother telling her that they were alone and would have to rely on each other. She did not attend her father's funeral. Her mother never talked about the details of the wreck, and Jill never asked, even though she often searched vainly for any memory of that night. The details of the wreck did not seem to matter but hearing her mother talk about the accident did. With her father dead, and her mother silent, she was alone.

She sat on a damp bench at the river's edge. The light of a distant streetlamp cast a rippling shadow on the water. She lowered her head. Raindrops dripped off the scant leaves drooping from the tree limbs that hung low above her bench and mixed with the tears that had begun to fall again. They fell together onto the warm, blue fabric of her faded jeans and widened into wet circles. She stared at the river as it flowed by, nearly invisible in the dark. She squeezed the tears from her eyes as her body began to shake with grief and cold. She hugged herself to steady the rising panic and to warm the dampness from her bones.

She began to rock back and forth on the bench. She tried to calm herself by imagining her father and conjuring up memories of a man who played with her and bought her books and toys and carried her on his shoulders. But nothing was vivid, nothing she could see clearly and certainly. It was as if a dense fog had rolled across her recollections, and without a clear picture of her past, she could not imagine a future.

The rain had stopped again, but the tears continued to stream down Jill's face as the surface of the river settled and flattened out. The Columbia remained the color of slate where the streetlights, which illuminated the asphalt pathway running north and south parallel to the river, did not shine on the dark water.

She stared at the current and felt a familiar and irresistible tug, a strong pull that seemed to extend from the depths of the channel to another place deep inside her. She resisted as she always did. But this time either the pull was too strong, or she was too tired, so she gave in.

She stood and walked carefully on the wet, downward slope to the river's edge until the quiet water soaked the toes of her shoes. The tears had stopped, and she stepped into the river. The cold shocked her awake, but she continued. Still in the light of the streetlamp, she felt the slow current nudge her downstream as the water reached her waist. She was completely in the dark by the time the water reached her chin. She inhaled and let the river take her away. It covered her head, and she stroked for the bottom. She turned over once and was surprised that the streetlight was dimly visible from beneath the surface. Tightness in her chest and a deep, burning sensation caused a sudden and unexpected sense of panic. Jill discovered she was struggling for the surface. She tried to find the river bottom, but when she pushed her feet down, it was not there.

She stroked for the surface, but her heavy coat made it nearly impossible to move her arms. The pressure of the water forced the oversized hood down against the top of her head and over her face, blocking the diminishing glare. Jill pushed the hood back off her face and struggled toward the streetlight. An image of her father flashed across her mind. He was frowning and seemed to be disappointed in her. A few moments before, she'd been standing on the riverbank and dying had seemed a welcome relief. Now terror and panic flooded her mind. Her lungs continued to burn, and the light continued to fade even though she strained to keep her eyes open. Finally, she felt herself drifting away. She reached once more for the surface, but she had no strength left. She ended the struggle that had begun the night her father died. The girl closed her eyes, and with a sob, exhaled and surrendered to the river.

Her body floated to the surface. The current banged her into a dock behind a new hotel on the riverbank. The force of the collision against her back turned her over and forced her to cough at the same time. Dark water burned her throat as it escaped her lungs. The girl reached out and grasped the dock with one arm. She reached up with the other arm and was able to get a hand around the thick rope that rimmed the edge. She rested there for several minutes before easing her way to the middle of the dock. A three-step ladder extended down into the water. Jill found the bottom rung with her left foot, and with a great effort, shrugged off the coat. She watched it sink as the current took it away. She put her right foot onto the next rung and stepped up and out of the river onto the dock. She was on her hands and knees, and her body was shaking when everything she had eaten during the day came up in one long eruption. Her head sagged toward the remnants of her junk-food lunch. The pungent, chemical odor of digestive fluid mixed with a badly chewed hotdog and a blue goo that had once been a blueberry Slurpee burned the inside of her nose. She retched again. When she was done, she rolled onto her back, away from the putrid puddle and felt light.

She stretched out and stared at the moon peeking through the thinning clouds. She closed her eyes and took in two or three deep, cool breaths, ecstatic that she could feel the damp river air flowing easily into her lungs.

✳✳✳

Everyone who lived in the desert near the Columbia in the days before the dams and the reactors had a river story to tell—of flood or fire or both. Stories of damnation or redemption. Occasionally of salvation. After her father died, Jill was irresistibly drawn to the river. She seemed to know that when the time came, the river would take away the pain of being alone.

When he was much younger than Jill, John Carpenter loved to travel to the river with his father from their home on the Roza, west of Benton City and midway up the slope toward Rattlesnake Ridge. They would journey on horseback through their scattered herd and across the sage prairie as it leveled out between the grassy rise of the ridge and the noisy progress of the Yakima River. To the north and west was the barren hulk of Rattlesnake Mountain, the tallest mountain in North America without a tree on it, or so a persistent local legend insists. The ride took most of an entire day and brought father and son to the sharp southern bend in the Yakima, where the ridge leveled into a broad plain three miles wide that stretched to the Columbia farther east.

In those days the Columbia was narrow and swift. The river had not yet been dammed to satisfy the thirst for water and the demand for power of people far distant from the desert and far removed from its life. At this southern limit of the Hanford Reach, John and his father would dismount, unsaddle, and let the horses graze on the moist, green grass that grew at the river's edge. They would fish and eat, but the river moved too fast for swimming. Still, the long ride was hot, so John would remove his clothes and wade naked into the current up to his thighs. The cold, rushing water carried away the heat and fatigue from his feet and legs. He'd lie down in the warmer water that eddied near the shore to cool his sunbaked skin.

The Columbia River was alive in those days, and the bank on both sides of the river was verdant and lush. The prairie stretched flat near the water's edge then up and away in all directions, brown and dusty in the summer heat. After a warm night on the riverbank, John and his father would saddle up again in the morning and ride home, back over the ridge or across the prairie and along the Yakima if the weather was hot. Some years later John explained the river's old flood cycle to a newcomer. "Twice some years in the old days, the Columbia spread out over its banks a mile on each side."

With the Columbia in flood, the Yakima seemed to shrink. After the dams went up, the Columbia did not flood and the surrounding countryside remained dry, but the semi-wild lower reach of the Yakima River retained its redemptive force and native cleansing power.

✳✳✳

Jill finally sat up. Her oversized clothes, khaki pants, and a thin, long-sleeve shirt clung to her narrow body, and her straight hair was stuck to the back of her shirt. She felt exposed without her long coat and without the protection of her hood, so she clutched her knees to her chest. She began to shake and shiver with terror and cold. She stumbled to her feet and walked stiffly up the ramp and off the dock. It was late, and the rain had stopped for good. She encountered several other kids walking along the paved path.

"Hey, it's the Creature from the Black Lagoon," one boy said then laughed.

Jill said nothing.

"Kind of cold for a swim, ain't it?" The boy said as he brushed by her. Several others laughed and ran off through the trees and into the park. She heard the roar of an engine starting and tires squealing as a car sped out of the park and back into town.

Jill hugged herself as the shivering increased. She headed through the park the same way the others had gone and stayed off the well-travelled streets. Within two blocks of her house, a green-and-white police car pulled up to the curb beside her. She did not stop, but a policeman got out of the car and began to follow her.

"Excuse me. Can I talk to you for a second?"

She stopped and turned toward the policeman who was several steps behind her. He was tall like her father. His face was familiar, and there was a gentleness in his voice that nudged a blurred image from the night of the wreck up from the depths of her memory.

"What did you say? I just thought..."

The policeman was next to her before she could continue. The chill was still with her, but she had stopped shaking. She kept her arms wrapped around herself as tightly as she could. She was determined not to let go.

"I'm on my way home, officer," she said.

"How'd you get so wet?"

Her mind seemed to have slowed down along with everything else. She did not answer right away. She trembled and said, "I fell in the river. I'm a little cold. I need to get home."

"Someone called us to say there was someone passed out on the float down there. Was that you? You look familiar. Do I know you?"

She did not answer.

"Do you need any help? How far away do you live? What do you need? A ride?"

Jill waited. "No. I live just down the street here. I'll go home and get warm."

"I better drive you. Get in."

"No, really, no."

She tried to run the last block to her house, but all she could manage was a stiff shuffle. The policeman got into his car and followed slowly. When Jill finally reached the walkway to her front door, the police car stopped at the curb again, and the officer followed her to the small porch.

"I'm okay now. Really. I just…"

"I better talk to your folks." He knocked on the door.

"Please. My mom's asleep."

"You look like you've had some trouble. I think I better have a talk with her. Is your father home?"

Again, Jill did not answer. She turned away from the door and leaned against the wall. She began to shake again. The damp air and her wet clothes seemed to merge.

"Please, officer, I'm okay. I don't want my mom woken up. She... she works all the time and...and I'm okay really. Please."

Jill was surprised when the man reached out and gently stroked her cheek. She flinched a little. But when he took his hand away, she remembered the warmth of her father's fingertips on a rainy day, a spot of relief from the cold. Again, the same indistinct image of her father crossed the girl's mind, and for an instant, while the memory remained, the cold dissipated.

"Well, okay, but if I were your dad, I'd want to know what happened. But you don't seem to be harmed much, just cold. Right?"

"Believe me, my dad won't care. And my mom needs her sleep."

"Alright, you go inside and get warm. Maybe I'll check on you in the morning."

"Thank you."

The policeman turned away, headed back down the narrow walkway, and got into his car. Jill had entered the house before he pulled away. On the couch, her mother was still asleep, just as Jill had left her. She was nearly undressed by the time she reached the bathroom. She piled her wet clothes in a heap outside the door and stepped into a scalding shower. She shuddered once then cried quietly. The hot water brought life back into her limbs as it rinsed the cold tears from her face. She let the water run over her for a long time before she got out and dried off.

She crawled naked into her small bed and pulled the blankets over her head to hide her face. She slept hard and for a long time.

And she dreamed.

The rain was coming down so hard she was having trouble breathing. She seemed to be a long way from home, but she was soaked and walking down the last block to her house. Finally, the policeman who had followed her home rescued her. But he was not in his uniform. He was dressed like her father on the night he died.

The dream woke her. She sat up and blinked at the glare from the streetlight outside her window and went back to sleep.

And she dreamed again.

This time the rain had stopped, and it was very hot. She was wearing the thick, hooded coat she had lost in the river. Though there was no sun in the dream, the heat was causing steam to rise from the coat. This time her father himself approached her.

"Don't be afraid, sweetheart. It's not so bad after a while."

When Jill woke up the sun was shining, and she could hear her mother moving about in the kitchen. For the first time in as long as she could remember, she felt rested. She kicked off the blankets and stretched. She got up, put on a thin robe, and walked into the kitchen.

"Mom?"

"How'd your clothes get so wet?"

"Uhhh..."

"Never mind. I've got a surprise. I think we need a change."

"A change? Mom?"

CHAPTER 4

John's heavily loaded truck groaned to the top of the last grade, and suddenly the Yakima Valley stretched out below. The flatbed picked up speed as it lumbered down a long hill and across the Fred G. Redmond Bridge, a surprisingly precarious span across a deep canyon, with the lights of Selah down the hill and to the right. John slowed the truck as it rolled onto the floor of the flat Yakima River Valley. They crossed the river for the first time with the lumber mill at Yakima on the right, its thousands of logs stacked in neat rows steadily soaked by noisy sprinklers.

A weak spotlight illuminated a fading red-and-white sign that said "Welcome to Yakima. Palm Springs of Washington." The sign seemed out of place to anyone who had ever been to Yakima. Most people in this corner of the country did not know much about Palm Springs, but they may have known rich people lived there, and rich people were not common in Yakima. There seemed to be way too many people who worked in the woods, fields, and orchards than there would be in Palm Springs. And besides, there were no lumber mills in the California desert.

During daylight along this stretch of Interstate 82, the Yakima River was occasionally visible to the left, behind dense clumps of damp willow trees, with Yakima to the right. Grady could not see the river at night, but he felt at home knowing it was nearby as they eased through the valley in the old truck. The Yakima River still flooded from time to time. When it did, this stretch of the interstate became river bottom. Cars and trucks had to be routed through Moxee and Sunnyside or all the way out to Hanford to bypass the flood waters.

The Yakima River began in a series of rippling streams and steep rapids on the high, western extremities of the eastern slopes of the Cascade Mountains. It snaked through deep canyons and slowed through a series of narrow valleys before it tumbled downward through the last canyon from Ellensburg to Yakima. There it flattened out for good. Water was pumped out of the river and sprinkled onto the orchards and vineyards on the steep hillsides between the valley and the Yakima's confluence with the Columbia a little downstream from Richland.

Even though the Columbia was the river that people in other parts of the country knew about, it was the Yakima River that watered the valley, and it was the Yakama Indians who lent their name to much of the region. The Columbia had been slowed and deepened and warmed by a series of dams from its source in British Columbia all the way to its urban demise downriver from

Portland at Astoria and Cape Disappointment. The Columbia and its sister tributary, the Snake, formed a watery highway bearing the abundance of the Inland Empire to the Pacific Ocean from as far east as Lewiston, Idaho.

But the Columbia never flooded anymore.

Upriver from Grady's destination—the government company town of Richland, Washington—was the Hanford Reach. The Reach was fifty miles long and the only free-flowing stretch of the Columbia left.

In the old days, the Columbia was big and wild, rushing out of the Canadian wilderness to carve an impressive gorge through the heart of the old Oregon Territory. It had forever been the region's Amazon, a western Nile, sacred to more than a dozen Indian tribes and worshipped for the abundance that once leaped from its rushing waters into grateful nets at places like Celilo Falls.

Grady dozed as John's old truck eased down the valley past Wapato and through the Yakama Indian Reservation at Toppenish. The interstate was never more than a couple of hundred yards from the Yakima. The highway crossed the river three times in sixty miles as the Yakima snaked its way toward the Columbia.

Grady was very tired. His fatigue and the stiffness that was showing up in his shoulders, the result of an awkward landing earlier in the day, made him think back. When he was a child, the most useful thing his frequently absent father had taught him was to accept his circumstances, especially once a thing was settled. Grady had grown into a taller, darker version of his father, a quiet man who had been a mostly successful rodeo cowboy, but in the rodeo world, being "most successful" meant he managed to earn back his fees and pay his expenses, and not much else. Grady wasn't even that well off the day John picked him up.

But there was something more, something tangible and solid, that continued to connect him to his father. It spanned both the years that separated father and son during the time the older man had been away and the miles that had kept them apart before he left. The connection had not weakened in the ten years his father had been gone, even though Grady rarely thought about it. When he did think about it, the boy resented his father's absence, but strangely his resentment was without rancor. He was regretful, not angry. Wistful rather than grieving. Instead of diminishing as the years passed, the connection to the man he knew as his father grew stronger when the boy began to ride bulls.

Now and then he'd run into a bull rider who had competed with his father. At such times there were always pats on the back and words of encouragement. And once, while he was checking his gear on a windy day in Goldendale, an old timer tapped Grady on the shoulder and said, "Son, did you know your daddy rode the same bull you've drawn today?" The revelation stunned him. As he settled down onto the back the old bull, he had the eerie sensation that he was in his father's place. The realization terrified him, and he was bucked off on the first jump.

Since then, Grady recognized the connection every time he climbed into the chute and onto the back of another bull. But he had never recognized the same familiar, bottomless terror that his father had known. Grady believed the terror was all his own, so it made him reckless.

Over the years an unreal quality regarding his father had developed in Grady's mind. An ethereal distance reinforced by time apart. The distance and the connection both seemed to have something to do with the fact that Grady's father grew up in the tiny hamlet of Benton City, at that time, a town where everyone seemed to know everyone else and was intimately interested in everyone else's business. That fact and the whispered accusations forced Grady's mother to move to Richland a year or two after his father had left for the last time. Grady never felt quite at home except when he returned to the smaller town, first with his mother to visit friends, and later when he drove himself to Benton City to learn rodeo from Hazard Quinn, the same man who had taught his father.

When he was younger and his father was newly gone, Grady's mother had to work two jobs to keep their little family together. So, the boy spent a lot of time by himself. When he got older his mother was able to work less, but by then Grady was spending as much time as he could learning to ride bulls and broncs from Hazard Quinn.

Quinn was a dusty, crusty, profane old man. No one knew precisely how old he was, but he was well into the early years of middle age when Grady's father begged him to teach him to ride bulls and broncs, and he was well along toward old age by the time

Grady came around with the same request. Quinn's method for choosing young riders was simple, and it never changed.

"Tell you what," he'd tell a youngster. "Ya'll come around here ever' day for a solid month and watch. Ever' day. Don't ask no questions and don't get in the way. If ya'll come here ever' day for a month. Then we'll just see about it."

Hardly anyone took him up on the offer. Some boys would show up for a week or two then give it up, but Grady's father came every day. He'd crawl up on the old arena fence and sit for hours watching thrill-seeking cowboys ride Quinn's practice bulls. Quinn had one rule. "If you get bucked off, and you can stand up on your own, you got to get on the next one. I don't care how bad it hurts. I ain't got time to waste if you're scared."

By the time Grady was ready to join Quinn's select group of young bull riders, Quinn was loved by no one and avoided by just about everyone except for a very small handful of young cowboy wannabes who hoped to glean his agile brain and years of experience for bits and pieces of rodeo wisdom. Quinn would say, "It ain't a matter of *if* you're goin' to get hurt, but *when*, and how bad. So, bein' afraid ain't goin' to do no good."

Grady sat up in the truck and pushed back his hat. They had gotten as far as Sunnyside, thirty miles from Benton City. John did not appear to have moved in the ninety minutes it had taken the truck to get this far.

"Almost there?" Grady asked, knowing the answer.

"Still almost an hour to my place. It'll be plenty late when we get there. Maybe you better come home with me and get some sleep. I got to go to town tomorrow, so I can take you to Richland then."

Grady was surprised by another generous offer from John, but he said nothing. The boy slid forward and leaned his head back against the seat. He pulled his hat down and went directly to sleep. And he dreamed. First, he saw his father on the back of a huge, white bull, his left hand waving in the air. In the dream, his father was waving to the young boy hanging on the arena fence while the man rocked back and forth effortlessly on the back of a gigantic bull that never bucked him off. Grady had a firm recollection of his father, a vision of faithfulness, love and strength, a memory that confused him because of the terrible thing the man had done. Grady knew the dream was not real, but even awake the boy could not recall a time when his father had been bucked off.

The truck groaned along the highway, and Grady's dream slowly shifted to his own ride earlier in the day, his hand high in the air like his father's, but for balance, waving at no one. He relived the sudden and momentary sense of panic that always rose in his chest just before he was dislodged. Suddenly, Grady's father was on the bull and the boy was flying through the air to land awkwardly. Then the rodeo clowns. Then he woke up in the truck.

"Where are we now?"

John's eyes stayed fixed on the dark strip of four-lane highway in front of him.

"Just past Prosser, I 'spect. Be to Benton City pretty soon."

"I guess I was tired."

"Yeah, you young fellas never feel tired, but then you're out like a light when the truck gets warm."

The hard rain had begun to fall again. The windshield wipers sloshed back and forth, and the road eased along the damp flat of the lower Yakima Valley.

"Were you serious about letting me stay with y'all tonight? I don't know why you'd want me at your place at all, what with my dad and your son...and I don't want to get in the way. Still, I don't really think I'd like to get my mom out in this weather. I guess I can pay a little if you need me to."

"That ain't necessary. I got cows to move in the morning before I go to town. If you can sit a horse better'n you rode that bull tonight, you can help out. That'll be pay enough."

"I can do that. But why are you doin' this? You got reason to hate me."

"I got no call to hate anyone. Maybe I thought I did once, but I've forgotten why. You ain't done nothin' to me. Maybe I even owe you a little somethin'."

Grady did not understand John's kindness, and he did not want to be indebted to him. But the old man had brought it up, and the chance to miss sitting out in the rain while he waited for his mother was more than he could pass up. He hadn't been on a horse that didn't buck for a long time, and he was growing curious.

The truck lugged through the rain the last seventeen miles from Prosser to the Benton City exit. The lights that marked the intermittent farms and the orchards on the north side of the highway became more and more sparse until Grady could see, through the steady drizzle, that the countryside was almost completely dark. The truck eased down a steep hill at last. The tiny town of Benton City gleamed through the rain-splattered side windows of the truck about a half-mile north of the highway. The illuminated boundaries of the town itself formed a rigid outline against the sparsely populated countryside.

As the highway began to slope down toward the Benton City off ramp, Grady knew the river was directly below them and to the left between the highway and the dim lights of the town. In the near distance, in front of the town and a little to the south, the lights of a Conoco station and minimart gleamed like an electric oasis in the darkness. Grady knew the owners were a former college football player and his wife, an amiable couple who would sell anything travelers on the interstate were likely to need or want—milk and eggs, fancy coffee, fancy magazines, a greasy meal, beer, and live bait.

In the summer palm trees lined the edge of the parking lot, and an aromatic barbeque sent irresistible smells wafting across the interstate on the breeze from the river. Grady suspected (and the owners were certain) that as many travelers were drawn to the Desert Oasis Mini-Mart by the barbeque as by the need to refuel.

John slowed the truck early to keep the load of hay from shifting forward, stopped at the foot of the off ramp, and turned left under the interstate.

"I better get some more diesel before I get through town," John said as he pulled the truck into a bright island of light next to the underpass. "Don't want to have to come this way tomorrow."

He pulled the truck into the fluorescent canopy of the gas station and got out to fill the half-empty tank. He walked around the truck, checking his load as he went. He took the diesel nozzle from the pump and began filling the cavernous gas tank behind the cab.

"I got to go inside for a minute," Grady said. His eyes hadn't quite adjusted to the bright lights as he went through the double doors. It was even brighter inside the minimart than it was outside under the canopy that covered the pumps. The rain had soaked the parking lot and was puddling up in low spots, making the glare from the overhead lights even more intense. Grady wondered if it was ever dark here. He walked the length of the store to the restroom near the back. The door was locked, so he leaned on the wall and waited.

Two young men about his age—one sockless in black Converse All Stars, cutoff jeans, and no shirt, and the other wearing a torn Olympia Beer tee shirt, faded Levis, and sandals—stood at the counter trying to buy beer. The boy in the tee shirt was wet up to his thighs.

"Can't sell you beer without some ID," the woman behind the counter said. "I'd get in trouble."

"Do I look like I'm under twenty-one?" The boy with the beer shirt growled as he slapped the counter with his open hand.

"Yeah, I think you do."

The restroom door opened and a middle-aged man in a disordered suit came out. He had the tired eyes of someone who had been on the road a long time.

"I'd wait a minute before I went in there." The man laughed and waved his hand in front of his face.

Grady didn't wait. When he came out, the two boys were still at the counter. He could see through the window in front of the store that John was still pumping gas and cleaning the road grime off the windshield. Country music blared from a small radio behind the counter, and on a TV set above a small "cafe" area at the front of the store, a game show host chatted with a fat woman in a flowery dress. He was suddenly aware that his head hurt. He squinted against the brightness in the store and started for the door.

"Hey, cowboy," one of the boys at the counter yelled after him. "You want a beer? You ain't going to get one from this ol' biddy."

The two boys pushed past Grady and shuffled through the door and toward the road. The boy in the tee shirt turned and flipped his middle finger at the woman behind the counter before he bolted for the dark road beyond the parking lot. Grady took one step out the door, grabbed the boy by the arm, and yanked him back against the brick facade of the building.

"Hey man, what do think you're doin'?"

"I think you should tell that lady you're sorry."

"Make me, cowboy!"

"Now!"

Grady turned the boy and started to push him into the store when the boy with no shirt came back to help. He grabbed Grady by the shoulders and tried to pull him away from his friend. But his heart wasn't in it. Grady shrugged him off and pushed the first boy back through the door.

"Tell her you're sorry."

"All she had to do was..."

"Tell her."

"Sorry."

"Sorry, ma'am!" Grady pushed him toward the counter, but when he did the boy twisted away and bolted through the door. He was cackling as he and his friend ran across the parking lot, turned right away from town, and ran across the road toward the river. Grady heard tires screech on the dark road, but no crash and no thud.

"I'm sorry, ma'am," he said. "But I can't stand it when guys act like that."

"Ain't your fault, honey. But there was two of them. You coulda been hurt."

"There ain't much they could've done."

"They're a regular pair of peckerwoods, ain't they?" The woman smiled. "They been in here before. They'll be back too...You look like you could use somethin' to eat, and maybe a cold drink? No beer though. You're no older than those two."

"Yes, ma'am. I ain't eaten all day."

The woman pointed to the refrigerators along one side of the store. Grady took two soggy sandwiches wrapped in cellophane and two Cokes. "Can I have one for my ride? He's brought me all the way from Ellensburg."

"Sure honey. You take care now, hear."

Grady left the store and climbed back into the cab of the truck. He put the sandwiches and Cokes on the seat and leaned back.

"Lord, I'm tired." He closed his eyes and waited for John.

When John returned to the truck, he shook off Grady's offer of a Coke, but accepted one of the sandwiches. He opened the cellophane slowly then placed it on the seat next to him. He eased the truck out of the gas station and turned left then right. He took a bite of his sandwich as they crossed a short steel suspension bridge that spanned the Yakima River and headed toward Benton City. Grady had already eaten half of his sandwich and was well on the way to finishing the second half by the time they were across the bridge. John wasn't particularly hungry, so he told the boy to eat the rest of his sandwich, an offer Grady accepted immediately and with gratitude.

The main street of the tired old town had few streetlights. The road into town was lined with trailers and old frame houses. Yards struggling in the name of civility alternated with small, fenced pastures kept green by generous irrigation. The grass was mostly for cows and horses, so lawns were small. The night Grady and John passed through was typical, with streets deserted after dark.

The only lights apparent along the one-street section of downtown Benton City came from the narrow windows of the Palm Tavern.

Benton City was one of the countless towns in the dry inland strip of the Pacific Northwest between the Cascade Mountains and the Rockies. These towns pushed back the sage desert and sandy prairie that stretched from northern California to the forests near the Canadian border in the upper reaches of the Columbia watershed. The citizens of their much larger neighbors in Richland and Kennewick often disparaged people in small towns like Benton City because they seemed grim. They seemed grim, because they worked hard for a living.

His mother moved Grady away from Benton City to Richland when he was barely twelve. But it was Benton City, nestled on the shore of a tight, northward bend of the Yakima River, where Grady and his parents lived when his father's rodeo travels allowed them to be together.

Grady was staring out the passenger-side window into the dark drizzle. He stuffed the last bit of sandwich into his mouth and swallowed it. He wiped his mouth with the sleeve of his shirt and flicked away a bit of white sandwich residue with his middle finger.

"I used to live here, and I've got people I know here still. I learned to rodeo here," he said. John was listening but said nothing because he already knew all this. "My mom and my dad and me. We lived down on the flood plain east of town close to the river. The house was built up a little, so we never got flooded.

The yard and the pasture flooded a couple of times, but the house was always dry."

John remained quiet. Grady seemed to be in some far-off place. He had never spoken aloud about those days, not even to his mother. The boy was surprised that he would speak so openly to John.

"I guess you know that my dad didn't leave exactly. He was taken away. I never knew where for sure. I heard stories after he left, and kids say stuff when they want to be mean. But he never came back. I'm pretty sure he was in jail for a while, so I guess it would be hard to come back here. Mom says it's better that we just get on with it and not think too much about where he is or if he's coming back."

John knew all this. "I reckon your mom's a smart woman. It's tough to get on with hard things, but once you're a mind to do it, I think it's best."

Grady heard John but did not respond. There was a peaceful quality about the old man, despite his rough look and the hard times he carried in his eyes, that peaceful quality made Grady continue.

"My dad taught me to ride when I was a little kid. I used to fall off a lot. We had a white pony when I was small. First time I got on him, the flank strap slipped back and slapped him behind his belly, and he bucked me off. I went straight up in the air and came down on my tailbone. Mom thought I'd broke it. It scared me a little, I guess, but I never really minded getting bucked off. Still don't."

"After seein' you try to ride that bull today," John said. "It's a good thing too."

Grady smiled. He was beginning to feel comfortable with John, and the comfortable feeling made him curious.

"Him and mom always seemed to get along fine, but he was tryin' to rodeo for a livin', and do ranch and farm work here and there when he wasn't rodeoin'. He was pretty handy, I think. He came home less and less often, 'til finally he didn't come home anymore at all. He sent us money, though. He sent money every time he won any. I remember that most of all. We could always use the money. Then the money stopped."

The truck was halfway through town now. The rain was letting up again. They passed the elementary school on the left, then the big, solid Baptist church, and the new high school behind neat athletic fields, and finally, they were out of town. The main street had become country road again, but straight rather than winding like it had been for the first mile off the highway. John drove on another two miles, past the markers in the soggy cemetery to Acord Road. He turned left and passed two or three solitary farmhouses set back off the road and surrounded by cherry orchards. After the first mile, the countryside became deserted. The road rose slightly for about half a mile until the pavement ended at an ancient wooden gate. The road on the other side of the gate was gravel and dirt and fell away steeply into a deep ravine.

John stopped the truck and started to get out to open the gate.

"Wait," Grady said. "I'll get it."

"You'll need the key. Here."

Grady slid out of the passenger-side door as the last raindrops hit the wet roadway. He easily found the padlock in the headlights. He had to struggle with the key before the gate finally fell open down the hill, and he had to run a few steps to keep it from getting away from him.

John drove the truck through the opening, and Grady wrestled the gate back up the hill and held it closed with his shoulder, so he could replace the chain and the padlock. As he was returning to the truck, he noticed one corner of the canvas tarp that labored to keep the hay dry was loose.

"Wait a minute," he yelled. "You got a knot loose." He pulled the orange bailing twine back through the brass grommet in the tarp, doubled it back on itself, and retied a hard knot. John would probably have to cut the twine to unload, but Grady didn't know how far they had to drive on the gravel road.

He climbed back into the truck and noticed the heat of the cab. He hadn't been cold in the short time he was outside, but the warm cab felt good just the same. John put the truck in gear, and the gravel road dipped sharply down to the right into a shallow ravine. Grady had heard of a swampy creek in the area, and he guessed it must be at the bottom of the ravine. The road ran along the floor of the ravine for about a quarter mile before it hair-pinned to the left over a narrow wooden bridge and up a steep hill. The truck's engine groaned under the heavy load at such a low speed. At the top of the hill, the road turned from gravel and dirt to wet dirt and mud. The truck slipped a little sideways in the mud on a sharp right turn.

"Ever get stuck up here?" Grady asked.

"Only once. And it was rainin' way more than today. The tires got to spinnin' under a big load of heavy posts. Good thing all three of my boys were home. They got on their horses and galloped out here right quick. They roped the bumpers and dragged her out, but the wheels spun some until I got on solid ground."

The truck did not get stuck this time, and John followed the flat road for another mile. It ended suddenly. John braked and turned down a narrow driveway and pulled up in front of a steel and wood barn about one hundred fifty feet from an old doublewide trailer.

"Here we are. I'll take you inside then check the stock in the barn real quick. It don't look like it's going to rain no more tonight, so I can unload this hay in the morning. It's not going to get any wetter if it does rain...Come on in the house. I'll get you settled in and then check the stock."

"I'll be glad to help."

"Nope. It'll only take a second. I got a couple a' yearling colts that get a might frisky when it rains and an old cow all penned up in the barn. That's all."

There was no porch light. But Grady could tell an old set of wooden steps led to the front door of the trailer. He wiped his boots hard on the well-worn welcome mat and followed John inside. A woman older than John, though Grady could not tell exactly how much older, sat in a wheelchair at a desk in one corner of the room. Her brown hair had developed generous streaks of gray, but her eyes were deep and bright, and she smiled slyly as John told her Grady was going to stay the night.

"Brought another one home, did ya," she said. "We got to start chargin' these younguns."

"This one says he can ride."

"Is that so?" the old woman said as her kind eyes surveyed Grady from head to foot.

"He says he's willing to help me unload the hay and move that little herd down from off the new fence in the morning."

"Well, that's a novelty," the woman said with a make-believe frown. "One a' these kids might be worth somethin'."

Grady stood in the middle of the worn carpet in the neat room with his hat in his hands. He was naturally nervous in the presence of strangers, and this old couple's kindness, especially the woman's snide patience, made him all the more anxious to earn their regard.

"This is Adah," John said, making a dismissive wave of his arm. "She don't do much around here except complain."

"Ma'am," Grady said.

"You look plumb wore out," John said. "I reckon a youngster like you needs his sleep. Woman, 'spose you can find this boy a bed?"

"We got a bed, alright," Adah said. "But it's still early. Son, you probably should eat somethin' first."

"Thank you, ma'am. But I already ate. John's right, though, I do feel a bit done in. That bull musta bucked me higher than I thought."

"Oh, Lord," Adah said. "You're a rodeo man, ridin' bulls too. I guess I misjudged you. You ain't likely to be all that useful after all. You go on, old man. Tend to those critters in the barn. I'll get young...what'd you say your name is? John never does mention a man's name until he's forced to."

"Grady, ma'am. Grady Cross."

Adah sat back and was silent for a time, but she did not take her eyes off Grady.

"Grady Cross at last." The old woman paused and bowed her head. "Land a Goshen. At last."

"What's that, ma'am?"

"Never mind, son. I was just thinkin' out loud...Where're ya'll from?" Adah asked, even though, like John, she already knew the answer.

"I live in Richland with my mom. We used to live out here, but that was before my dad..."

"Before your daddy left you all high and dry, right? It's an old story. We don't hold it against you, or him neither I don't 'spect. Come on now. It's getting to be mighty late for us old folks. Your room's at the end of the hall."

Adah removed the heavy shawl she had draped over her lap and folded it neatly on the floor. She put her hands on the big wheels on either side of her chair and began to roll across the room and down the hallway with surprising speed. She arrived at a door at the far end of the hall before Grady had time to collect his riggin' bag and follow her.

"Well, come on now. It's gettin' later all the time. John did say you'd help us out in the morning."

"Yes, ma'am. I'm comin'."

Grady walked quickly down the short hallway and entered the room. Adah had cleared some books and odds and ends of clothing off the bed. She pointed to a bathroom next door. Get some rest. We won't wake you up too awful early. Make yourself at home."

"Ma'am, do you know who I am?"

Adah did not answer immediately.

"Ma'am?"

"Son, I reckon you're a young man needin' a place to sleep. And we got such a place. I guess that's all I need to know about you." She paused and spun her chair around. Over her shoulder, she said, "Maybe we'll have a talk in the morning."

CHAPTER 5

Grady wasn't sure of the time, but it felt late in the morning, and the house was silent. He walked to the window, moved the faded curtain aside, and peered out. The sun sat higher than he thought it should be if he was going to help John. He pulled on his boots then retrieved his black hat from the foot of the bed and rushed out of the room. He found Adah sitting in her chair in the small kitchen vigorously mixing something doughy in a glass bowl she held against her body.

"Well, well. We was gettin' worried. Anyone that sleeps this late might ought to move to town. Ain't going to be much use out here." Adah punctuated her remarks with a slight grin and a hint of mischief. Grady wasn't sure how to react.

"Oh well, I reckon a free hand gets to say when he gets up," she said. "Even if most a' the work'll be done by the time he gets around to it."

"I'm sorry ma'am, I..."

"Don't pay her any mind, youngun. She's just sassy 'cause she can't walk too good or do much a nothin' else anymore." John had come into the kitchen from outside just as Grady started to speak. "I haven't done nothin' but feed the saddle horses and check on the colts in the barn corral. I won't be ready to go after those cows for a while."

John stepped in close behind Adah's chair and bent over and kissed her softly on top of the head. He straightened up and sent a sidelong smile in Grady's direction. "Woman, give this boy some breakfast so he can be of use later on."

"Maybe this young feller don't think a little ride in your old truck is worth a day's work driving cows. Maybe he'd like to get on home."

"No, ma'am," Grady surprised himself with his quick answer. "I sure do appreciate the ride and the bed, and I'd really like to help with those cows if I can."

"I know, son. When you get to be our age, sassin' each other's about all you got."

John went back outside. Adah placed the mixing bowl on the low counter and turned her chair toward Grady.

"I'll get you some breakfast."

She loaded eggs, ham, and big chunks of homemade bread soaked with butter onto a heavy porcelain plate. She set the food on the table and motioned for Grady to sit and eat. Then she spun her chair around, retrieved the mixing bowl, returned to the table, and continued to stir the doughy mixture.

"My mom used to make breakfast like this when my dad was home," Grady said. "Ma'am, I feel like I've gone back to when by dad was...Well, I can't remember the last time I've had breakfast like this. Seems like I've gone back in time."

"That's sorta what we intend, son. Me and John haven't quite figured out what's so fine about the present time. His daddy got a lot of money from the government back in the war. Sold off about two-thirds of this place for more'n it was worth and used the money to pay off the rest.

"They was building all that bomb nonsense over to Hanford and wanted as much of the land around here as they could get. John don't seem to care to get rich, so he never tried to keep up like some of the other ranchers, the ones from the old days. Most of those fellers sold out to the big orchard outfits and moved to town. John don't have to make much on his cows to break even, so he can go along doing things the way he always has, the way he likes. We don't have much money, but we do got the long ago to fall back on."

She lowered her gaze into the mixing bowl and was silent for a long moment.

Grady looked up from his breakfast. "Ma'am?"

She balanced the mixing bowl carefully on her lap and looked up at him. "Yes, son, what is it?"

"Why'd y'all put me up here last night? I've gotten lots of rides home from rodeos, but no one ever offered to give me a bed and a meal. And there's my dad. I know he..."

"Oh, you'll earn the bed and the meal, I reckon."

"No ma'am, excuse me, but you and John have been awful kind to me already. And you got plenty of reason not to be. Even the work this morning is a kindness. I can ride a bull or a bronc, but I ain't no workin' cowboy. I can sit a horse all right, but I've hardly ever seen a cow that wasn't in a rodeo pen. Why do y'all do it?"

Adah leaned back. She pushed both hands hard against the arms of her wheelchair and closed her eyes. Though she seemed like she was asleep, her hands returned to cradling the mixing bowl. When she finally spoke, she looked away from Grady. He could not tell if she had opened her eyes.

"You're not the first. John manages to pick up a boy like you ever' coupla months, more in the summertime. You're all about the same age. All dressed the same. Hat, boots, Wranglers unless they didn't know no better, and John won't give a youngster a second look if he ain't wearing the right kinda boots."

She turned toward Grady with her eyes open and frowned. "Most ain't so lean, though. Some are hitchhikin', trying to get home somewhere. But a fair number have been rodeo men.

"He brings 'em home. I don't mind. None of the boys has been any trouble. He's kinder than he needs to be, but I reckon John has a need to do a young man a kindness from time to time. You know his son died and you know how. He was about your age when he was killed."

"John told me that, but that's all he'll say. It's like we both know the truth, but neither can quite say it."

"I don't talk about how that boy died. But I know the truth is what it is. It ain't nothin' else, and it ain't usually what most folks think. You may learn more if you stay around long enough. John and you've crossed paths before, but he never bothered to bring you home. The time wasn't right."

"What's changed?"

Adah looked away and closed her eyes again. He thought he saw a brief pain cross her face. She was perfectly still for a moment and then said, "Maybe that old man has changed. A body can't bear the load he's been carryin' for all these years, not forever and not alone. Maybe he's ready to put it down and let someone else carry it."

"Me?"

"Somebody else. I reckon we'll have to see who."

"What about those other boys?" he said. "You said he's brought other boys out here."

"Yes, but you're the first one that's taken him up on his offer to work. I think it's 'cause he always means for the boys to get on a horse. A lot of the time, they look like cowboys, but they don't know which end of a horse to clean up after."

"Like I said, ma'am, I can ride a horse, but I'm not likely to be that much help."

"It's not help he's after, son. It's time. The time he missed with his own boy. Maybe it's the time you've lost. I think he holds hisself to account for what happened to his son...and maybe to you too. You're the one doing the kindness today, by agreein' to stay and ride out after them cows with him."

Grady hadn't meant to get the old woman to tell so much.

"Why are you telling me this, ma'am?"

"No one else ever asked. You leave it alone for a spell. Help John with his cows. Listen to what he has to say. We've been waitin' for some considerable time for you to show up here." She seemed to snap back to the present moment. "That's enough for now. You go on and eat."

Adah wheeled the chair around and rolled quickly out of the kitchen and down the hall, leaving the boy to finish his breakfast, which he did.

***

Grady left the house through the back door and walked out to the barn. His back hurt, his shoulders were tight, and a spot throbbed on his left hip. The bull in Ellensburg had gotten closer than he realized.

He walked to the small wooden corral in front of the barn. He grabbed the top rail of the corral fence with both hands, pushed his feet forward, and leaned back hard to stretch his back and shoulders. He felt the stiffness turn into a therapeutic pain as the deep stretch began below his neck and then moved down his shoulder blades and into the small of his back.

"You're way too young to feel the way you look," John spoke from the other side of the corral. "Climb on up here and let's get goin'."

"What about the hay on the truck?"

"My oldest boy, Frank, he'll be by to unload it while we bring the cows down."

Grady wasn't sure if he'd like to meet John's son, but he said nothing.

John was sitting on a smallish gray gelding leaning on the saddle horn. A heavy pair of scratched chaps covered the same old jeans he'd worn the day before. Grady thought that if John saw the need for chaps, he might wish he had a pair before they were done.

Next to John and the gray horse, a stocky bay mare stood quietly under a cumbersome, old roping saddle. A strip of an old inner tube wrapped around the tall horn. A leather strap secured a neatly coiled lariat to the saddle. John held the horse by a single rein. He handed Grady the rein as the boy walked around the corral and in through the open gate. Grady threw the rein over the horse's neck and the mare skittered a bit sideways when the thick leather slapped against her shoulder. He looked up nervously at John who was smiling at the boy's unease.

"Don't worry she won't dump you...more'n once."

"I surely do hope we don't have to rope anything," Grady said as he reached out to steady the stirrup. He had to stretch up on his right toe to get his left foot into the stirrup. He grimaced as he gathered the reins and pulled himself up with the saddle horn. He grunted a little as he swung his right leg over the mare's back. The horse began to walk away before he was fully seated, and Grady had to lean back quickly and tug on the reins to get her to stop.

"Whoa there, girl. We're not quite ready yet." Grady got the horse settled, stretched his heel down a bit, and stood up to test the length of the stirrup. Everything seemed to fit okay.

"I learned to ride pretty good when I was little, but I can't remember the last time I was on a horse that wasn't trying to buck me off."

"Go light on the reins, son. She won't give you any trouble as long as you stay out of her mouth, but when we start up some steeper stretches of the trail, you'd best get a hold of her mane or the horn 'cause she'll get you to the top in about two jumps."

"Where are we headed?"

John pointed with his chin toward the steep slope of Rattlesnake Ridge to the north.

"Two or three miles straight that-a-way. We'll gather up a small herd of cows and half-grown calves that's grazing at the base of the ridge and bring 'em back down here. Put 'em in the pasture behind the barn and they'll be able to graze all the way down to the river. It's kinda like fall roundup in the old days. But this'll only take a few hours. I don't have so many cows anymore, and mostly they stay close together."

John squeezed the gray horse with his calves and moved off, through the gate and away from the corral. Grady waited a few seconds and watched the old man ride off before he gave the mare a light squeeze with his calves. She stepped away, moving at a gentle trot until she caught up with the gray horse then settled in beside John. Grady could see all the way to the top of the ridge and could even make out the scattered red dots that were John's mostly Hereford cattle. They grazed halfway up the gentle slope.

An hour later they were two miles north of the house near a long fence line, at the point where the upward glide that begins at the Yakima River soars steeply toward the crest of Rattlesnake Ridge. The ridge runs to the northwest for about two miles before it races upward one more time toward the long peak of Rattlesnake Mountain, three thousand feet above the valley floor.

"My dad owned everything from the river to the top of the ridge," John explained. "But the government came along in '43 and '44 and bought everything from this fence here up over the ridge. Part of all that mess over at Hanford."

Grady knew a little about Hanford, how in the 1940s the government needed a place to build components for the first nuclear bombs. Three small towns were bought out, and two of the towns, Hanford and White Bluffs, became part of the Hanford Nuclear Reservation. The people had to go somewhere else, so the third, Richland, became a government-company town. Richland became the headquarters for the project and the population boomed from a few hundred people to more than forty thousand in less than a year.

"I was pretty young in those early days after the war," John said. "Had an uncle who left our place and went to work at Hanford. He never came back out here. Died of cancer in Richland in '59. We never knew if it was cigarettes or the bombs."

Below John and Grady forty or fifty cows grazed, most with lanky early spring-born calves close by. The cattle were spread out for more than half a mile on the sage prairie that sloped back toward the house and after that to the Yakima River. The advancing morning had become warm, but a westerly wind blew along the slope and caused Grady to shiver and pull up his collar John didn't seem to notice the wind or the chill.

"You work from down at that end," he told Grady, pointing off to the west. "I'll go down to the other end and we'll gather 'em up in the middle and drive 'em real slow down toward the home place. They'll bunch up and drive easy, I 'spect. They've done this before."

Grady was surprised that the stiffness and soreness from getting bucked off into the mud the night before had begun to ease as he got used to the easy movement of the old mare.

"I don't know why I do it this way anymore," John said stretching his back and gazing hard across the valley at the Horse Heaven Hills on the other side of the river. Grady let his eyes follow John's gaze. The house was visible in the middle distance. Brief stretches of the Yakima River were also visible where the valley wall flattened out. But John's eyes seemed to be level. Beyond the river was the new concrete of Interstate 82 with cars grinding by in both directions.

Above the new highway, the Horse Heaven Hills rose to the south, a wall of sage brush and silence. Far away in that direction

Grady knew the Columbia River had turned west to flow toward Portland and the Pacific Ocean. He turned and looked to the north, up Rattlesnake Ridge. To the northeast, the ancient prairie rolled away toward the Hanford Nuclear Reservation.

At Hanford, a generation of scientists and technicians had labored to slow the progress of several million gallons of nuclear sludge that had begun to seep into the rocky ground from aging underground tanks. The nuclear poison was pulled by gravity and squeezed by the inexorable weight of the Earth toward the Columbia. Among the new tribe of scientists and engineers who had come to clean up the radioactive mess, the history of the region began with Leslie Groves and the Manhattan Project, and included only Hanford, the reactors, and the leaky tanks. But John could remember a time before the reactors when he and his father could ride fifteen miles across the dry, unfenced prairie to the green banks of the big river. Time would end for the Columbia if the deadly remnants of forty years of plutonium production ever reached the river.

Grady turned back, and John was still gazing off into the high distance above the Horse Heaven Hills. He sensed the nuclear reality of Hanford was already in the past for John. The old man sat silently on his horse with his cattle and the rocky land spread out below him with his home in the near distance. Grady leaned back in the saddle and stretched his stiff legs down against the stirrups. When he sat up again, he felt calm, and for an instant, time did stand still.

"I don't reckon these cows are going to move themselves," John said as he reined his horse off to the east. Grady tugged lightly on his own reins and nudged his mare off to the west. They'd herded the cows into a tight group after an hour. Two hours later John had driven the cows back to the home place at a slow walk while Grady trailed along to one side trying to be useful by keeping the herd pointed south.

When they reached the home place, a man much younger than John held open a wide gate. The cows moved easily through the gate and spread out south of the barn. In another few hours, they would work their way down to the valley floor and graze along the Yakima River. John knew the cattle would move back closer to the barn when he put hay out during the winter and then return to the riverbank to calve in the early spring. The Yakima rarely froze, so water was plentiful all year.

Grady was sore again and very tired. He leaned forward in the saddle to take the pressure off his back. The leather fenders of the old saddle had rubbed his knees nearly raw.

"Looks like you got yourself a real cowpoke there, Dad."

John smiled. "He did all right."

"All he'd have to do is stay on that mare and she'd follow those cows down the hill okay."

"That's about the way it went," Grady said. He climbed down from the horse, stepped awkwardly to the ground, and nearly stumbled forward when he discovered his knees wouldn't quite straighten out. He handed the reins to John and rolled his shoulders forward and back to stretch the muscles in his neck.

"That's my son," John said. "The oldest. He used to think he could sit a horse and rope pretty good. Frank. Grady."

Frank was at least four inches taller than Grady's six feet. He took Grady's hand when he offered, squeezing softly.

"Grady Cross?" Frank increased his grip slightly and did not let go. "Didn't you used to live out here with your momma and daddy when you was a kid, six maybe seven years ago?"

"That's right."

The two young men stared at each other without speaking. Frank nodded, released Grady's hand, and looked toward John. He removed his battered straw cowboy hat and ran his nervous fingers through his hair and began to stammer.

"I used to know...My brother...I... I got to tell you...Dad, what is he doing here?"

Grady said nothing, but he felt his right fist clench. He started to take a step toward Frank, but John stepped between his son and Grady.

"Me and this young feller got to get into town, Frank. Why don't you put the horses away for us?"

Frank shook his head and slapped his hat against his thigh. "Well then, maybe I don't got nothin' much to say."

Frank took a step backward and put his hat back on. He took both sets of reins from his father and continued to watch Grady.

"There's no need to drive those cows that way anymore," Frank said. "But this old man's stubborn about things."

Grady felt his right hand relax. "John says you're a roper."

Frank did not want to respond. But after a long pause, he spoke quietly with his eyes diverted. "I don't rope much no more. Don't get much call for it 'cept at rodeos."

Frank held a set of reins in each hand. He pulled lightly on the rein in his left hand so the mare Grady had ridden would step in closer to him. He shifted both sets of reins to his left hand and reached up and absently began to rub the old horse between the ears. The old mare half-closed her eyes and dropped her head a few inches to make it easier for Frank to rub the tension out of her forehead. She sighed.

"Adah said there's a boy here who'd tried to ride a bull at Ellensburg yesterday. That must be you," Frank said. He pursed his lips and stared at Grady, but Grady found no anger in his eyes, only deep sadness. "I 'spect you got dumped, right?"

"Yeah. I did. Came down hard."

Frank's face softened. "Well, that's the way it is sometimes. Sometimes people go down hard." He turned away abruptly, and Grady watched as he led the horses back to the barn.

John moved off toward the house and the promise of another big meal, but Grady did not follow. The long ride seemed to help loosen his tight muscles, but his back still ached, his hip still hurt, and he felt uneasy about Frank. He turned away from the direction Frank had gone with the horses, and glancing back to the north, he could see where they had come with John's red cows. A little to the east, where the ridge curved toward the plain that separated the Yakima River from the Columbia, a luminous, white cloud rose straight up, as if from the floor of the desert, and spread out ominously, forming a nearly perfect mushroom. Grady knew the cloud was steam from the giant cooling towers at one of the Hanford reactors. He had seen the cloud before but had never stopped to watch it ascend, spread out, and dissolve into the atmosphere.

CHAPTER 6

After another big meal in Adah's kitchen, John drove Grady into Richland. Going even short distances in eastern Washington seemed like time travel. Geologists say the region's unique landscape was created over a period of 2,000 years. An Ice Age dam at the head of a deep river valley near present-day Missoula, Montana failed repeatedly, and each failure released several cubic miles of water. The series of watery cataclysms gouged a series of deep canyons across eastern Washington, rippled the valley floors and drilled dozens of enormous potholes. The result was a strange topography comprised of seemingly endless miles of a landscape hardly changed in the twelve thousand years since the most recent Missoula Flood. This primitive landscape was dissected by asphalt ribbons that meandered among the endless hills, interrupted infrequently by small settlements and a few larger towns. John appreciated the uninhabited nature of the region and often avoided the interstate. He drove Grady to Richland, north away from Benton City along the free-flowing Yakima River.

Like most other small towns in eastern Washington, Benton City had not changed much since the middle of the last century. The pace of life was deliberately slow and the people were generally quiet and without extraneous ambition. But Richland had been possessed by a confident cult of technological progress ever since the first scientists and engineers arrived at the Hanford Nuclear Reservation in the 1940s. Most of the highly educated, well-compensated scientists and engineers who formed the backbone of the workforce at the Hanford site lived in Richland. A musty regional joke said that the plumber who lives next door to the nuclear scientist in Richland thinks he's smarter than other plumbers because he lives next door to the nuclear scientist. The locals did not concern themselves with the subtle nuclear danger because "There's a lot of really smart people workin' at Hanford."

John drove slowly north and east along the Yakima by the same route he and his father had once taken on horseback. The river narrowed here, and the valley walls steepened with the sudden slope of Rattlesnake Ridge running away to the northwest on the left and the precarious walls of a brown mesa across the river on the right. Invisible on the mesa's flattop were several large circles of green alfalfa and golden corn. A modern drip irrigation system moistened the crop land. The system was designed to preserve every possible precious drop of water sucked from deep beneath the arid countryside. On the other side of the valley, Rattlesnake

Mountain had been crowned by a modern stellar observatory placed at the peak of the aged land, so men of the future can gaze toward heaven and peer confidently back into time. The extreme topography made the land on each side of the river undesirable for any use other than occasional grazing by a transient herd of cattle. Except for the narrow roadway, the final slow miles of the Yakima River remained an unchanged and substantial link to the valley's gratefully remembered past.

"I appreciate all this," Grady said, after he and John had driven half of the twenty miles from John's place to Richland.

John put his hand up. "It ain't much. I reckon everyone my age has been about where you are right now, more than once. It's not so much kindness as payback, I guess."

"Payback for what? I'd think you'd want payback from me."

"When I was young, older than you, but still young in most ways, I bought a horse at the auction in Toppenish. A nice little sorrel gelding. Three years old. Nice hip. Pretty head. The auctioneer said he was broke to ride, and they like to tell the truth when they know it. When they don't, they usually don't say nothin' at all.

"Anyway, I looked this colt over in the pens before the sale. And I figure if I could get him for around five hundred dollars, I might ride him for a couple of months and then turn him over, sell him to someone else and make a couple of hundred bucks. He looked to be a nice horse.

"I went back and forth with one other bidder for a while and finally got him for five hundred seventy-five. I was pleased with myself. When I was leaving the auction barn, a woman grabs my arm and says real quiet, 'That horse is sore in the back end. That's why they're selling him.' I was surprised. This lady knew something I didn't, and suddenly my good horse seemed like a waste of money, and I didn't even have him in the trailer yet.

"Well, I swallowed hard and went down to pay for the horse. When I was done, a man came up to me and said 'I was the other bidder on that horse. Did you know he has a jack? He's pretty much lame. He'll be sore most of the time.' I asked him what he would have given for him, and he said five hundred dollars. Then he said the strangest thing anyone's ever said to me: 'Call me after you get him home. I'll trade you for somethin' that's sound.' In the end I found out that man and that woman in the auction barn were together, and she had a nice two-year-old filly she wanted a thousand dollars for. She took that gelding and five hundred for her filly. I didn't make any money, but I ended up with a good horse."

"Why?"

"The man and the woman said they didn't want to see anyone get cheated. I paid too much for a horse that wouldn't be all that useful and those people took it on themselves to fix my problem. I don't know what they had planned for the horse they got from me, but I'm sure they lost money on the deal. Was it kindness? Of a sort, I suppose. I was a stranger to them, and I've never seen 'em since."

"Good Samaritans?"

"Strangers for sure. That filly turned out to be the best horse I ever owned. You rode one of her babies out after them cows this mornin'. I've been real careful ever since to make sure I don't sell a horse that ain't going to be useful to the buyer."

Grady leaned back and covered his eyes with his forearm.

As John's old truck grunted over the crest of a small hill and headed down toward the last bridge across the Yakima River, all three of the Tri-Cities were visible. Richland, the prosperous government company town, stretched between a three-mile shelterbelt above the steep banks of the Yakima River and the park-like Columbia River shore. Pasco had been the region's only substantial city in the years before World War II, but now the gritty old town hunkered down on a dusty flat near the confluence of the Columbia and Snake rivers. And Kennewick, which had never quite outlived the hard edge of its working class roots, sprawled gray and grim across the Columbia from Pasco and across the Yakima from Richland.

John left the highway and slowed the truck on the long, circular off ramp and followed Grady's directions to a house two streets from where Jill and her mother lived. John parked the truck along the curb in front of the house. Grady was surprised his mother's small car was not in the driveway. He hurried up the concrete walk and peered through the front window. He tried the doorknob, but the front door was locked. He took a key from the watch pocket of his Wranglers and unlocked the door.

Inside, the house was tidy, but the air was hot and stuffy, and all the lights were off. Grady walked through the kitchen and down a short hall to his mother's room where the bed was neatly made. In the closet most of his mother's clothes remained, but the one suitcase she owned was missing. He left his mother's room and hurried down the hall to his own room.

Outside in the truck, John leaned back and pulled his hat down over his eyes. He often dozed when he waited in the pickup. The autumn sun had warmed the cab, and sleep was an easy indulgence. His thin chest rose and fell slightly as he dozed. He dreamed of a day not so many years back when Frank and Robert, John's middle boy, had just won the team roping in a small rodeo at Wiley City near Yakima. The two young men were sitting in the stands with John watching his youngest son, Charlie, win the calf roping on a spotted horse named Gunner. John was fond of this particular dream, because it was the only time all three boys had won their events in the same rodeo. The memory was pleasant, but John's dream never included what happened after the rodeo. Since Charlie was well below legal age, the boys planned to spend the early evening celebrating loudly in a grocery store parking lot next to a tavern in Wiley City. The celebration ended abruptly when Frank was unable to prevent Charlie from picking a fight with a dusty steer wrestler who refused to be impressed with the boy's victory in the calf roping. After the steer wrestler knocked Charlie nearly unconscious, and before Frank and Robert could get organized to retaliate, John herded all three boys into the truck. They passed a speeding police car going in the opposite direction as they headed back toward the rodeo grounds to retrieve their horses.

John's dream was cut short by a loud thumping noise. The biggest of three teenage boys, who had been walking by on the sidewalk, had slapped the door of the truck, waking him.

"Hey cowboy, wake up," the boy yelled, tapping on John's window. "Someone stole your horse."

Back in the house, Grady found an envelope on the pillow of his bed. Inside was a note from his mother. He read it slowly:

Grady,

I got a call from your father. He wants to see me. I'm going to Walla Walla to see what this is about. He sounded hurt, but it's been so long, I can't tell. I'll call when I can. Stay close to the phone.

Love,
Mom

"Walla Walla?" he said.

He crumpled the note and felt his chest tighten. A vague burning sensation began in his stomach and rose to the back of his throat. He straightened the paper and read the note again. Then he folded it carefully and put it back in the envelope. He bent the envelope in half and stuffed it into the back pocket of his jeans. He went to a small desk in the front room and tugged on the large drawer to the left of a wooden chair that he flipped out of the way. The chair turned upside down, slid across the room, and crashed against a rickety cabinet that held a small television and his mother's very old phonograph. As usual, the drawer was locked. Grady stomped into the kitchen and found a long screwdriver in a box on a shelf above the refrigerator. Back at the desk, he knelt and jammed the screwdriver into the tiny space at the top of the drawer and began to pry. In a few seconds the lock broke, and Grady yanked the drawer open. In it were dozens of envelopes gathered into several bundles, each held together with a rubber band. Each was addressed to his mother and contained a letter from his father. Grady was not interested in the letters, only in the return addresses and postmarks. He pulled several letters out of the drawer. The return addresses were all the same. The most recent was postmarked one week earlier.

Grady Cross Sr.
Inmate No. 830707
Washington State Penitentiary
Walla Walla, Washington

He sat back on his heels.

"Prison? I thought he was out a long time ago. Then it's true... John's son." He stared at the same return address and postmark on another envelope. Then another. His mother had received a letter once a month for six years.

Grady breathed in hard, trying to cool the hot rage rising his body. He pushed it back down and let it settle while he rubbed his face with both hands. He hadn't shaved since before the Ellensburg rodeo, and the adolescent stubble prickled the skin on his cheeks. He thought for a moment, forcing himself to breath slowly to round off the sharp edges off his anger. He slammed the drawer shut. The desk tipped back hard and banged against the wall. A reading lamp teetered on the edge of the desk and crashed to the floor as Grady headed for the front door.

When he came out of the house, he saw the three boys standing near John's truck. The tallest tapped on the window, and John pushed the door open. But when he started to get out of the truck, the tall boy tried to slam the door closed again. Grady ran across the lawn, grabbed the boy by the shoulder and spun him around. When the tall boy was facing Grady, he said, "What the ...?"

He put both hands on Grady's chest. When the boy tried to push him away, Grady slapped his arms aside with his left hand, twisted back and hit the boy hard in the face with his right. Grady felt a satisfying crunch as the bones in the boy's nose and cheekbones splintered and cracked beneath his fist. The tall boy's knees buckled, and he sank quickly to the sidewalk and slumped forward onto his hands and knees. Dark red blood flowed from his nose and formed a crimson puddle on the sidewalk. Grady kicked him twice in the ribs. He paused when the boy fell onto his side. With his chest heaving, Grady saw that John had gotten out of the truck and was watching him closely. He had one hand on the chest of one of the other boys, holding him at arm's length. John shook his head and looked away, and Grady kicked the tall boy again. The boy grunted loudly. He held himself still with his left hand pressed against his right side, leaving Grady to think that his last blow might have broken at least one of the boy's ribs.

One of the other boys made a half-hearted attempt to push Grady away, but Grady hit him in the left eye with his right fist, and the boy stumbled backwards. He turned on the third boy, who had stepped away from John.

"You next?"

"Hey, no way, man. We were just playing around."

"Go play somewhere else."

The third boy helped his bloodied friend to his feet. His dirty tee shirt was soaked with blood, and he was holding his nose with his right hand and his ribs with his left. "Let's get out of here. Your nose is all busted up."

"You're in a load of trouble," The tall boy could barely speak through the blood that continued to flow from his nose.

The three boys headed up the street in the same direction they'd been going. Grady watched them disappear around a corner. John was back in the truck with the driver's side window down.

"Get in the truck, boy."

Grady walked around the front of the truck, opened the passenger-side door, and stepped up into the passenger seat. He rubbed his knuckles and noticed they had already begun to swell.

"You ought not to of done that, son. They didn't mean much harm."

"I know."

Grady stretched his back, slumped down, and leaned his head back against the seat of the truck and closed his eyes. "My dad's been in prison in Walla Walla. My mom's gone to see him. She's been lyin' to me all this time. I thought he was out years ago and just didn't want to come home. She said he had to go away. She told everyone he just went away. She never said where exactly, but now I guess I know why. You know why too, John. Just say it."

John started the engine, pushed in the clutch, and jammed the old truck into gear. "I ain't going to talk about this no more."

Grady looked up in surprise. John drove down the street and out of Richland, and they returned to the ranch in silence. Grady noticed the blood from the tall boy's nose on the knuckles of his right hand. He tried to wipe the blood off on his jeans, but it was still damp and smeared up the back of his hand toward his wrist. Tiny droplets of splattered blood stained the right sleeve and front of his shirt. Two of the three snaps that held the cuff of his shirt closed had come loose during the fight. Grady was perfectly calm as he snapped the cuff shut. He stared at his knuckles but felt nothing for the boy whose blood stained the back of his right hand and the front of his shirt. He turned both hands over and looked at his palms, and his hands began to shake. He took two or three shallow breaths and thought of his father's long absence. He squeezed his temples with his fists and bit down hard with his back teeth. His eyes burned.

Grady felt utterly alone.

"Six years in prison? All this time," he said to himself. "Why didn't Mom tell me the truth? I thought he got out and then just up and left. I thought he would be able to come back someday. I thought..."

John remained silent. He continued to stare straight ahead. Grady let out a long, anguished groan and began pounding the dashboard of the truck with both fists.

***

The stars gleamed. Grady peered into a night sky so clear that each star seemed to blink from its own particular place in the universe.

"It's somethin' ain't it, all them stars, and ain't one of 'em the same as any other." Adah had wheeled herself down a ramp at the back door and onto a sturdy board path that carried her out onto the edge of the yard where Grady stood beyond the lights of the house. She surprised him, and he jumped a little on the inside.

Adah stood up slowly and steadied herself with one hand on back of her chair and the other on Grady's shoulder.

"Ma'am?"

"I been watchin' a show on TV about stars and the universe. Scientists say they can figure back to within an instant after the universe exploded into bein'. Things down here usually get exploded out of bein'." She laughed.

"I don't know, ma'am. Mom used to take me to church and the preacher, and the Sunday school teachers all used to talk about creation and how God did it all in seven days. Then at school they'd tell us about stars and how long it takes light to get from there to here. I just don't know. I don't suppose it matters much."

"Oh, I reckon God's big enough for all that alright. And it does matter."

Grady stretched his back and rubbed his sore knuckles. Adah didn't move except to raise her eyes. She stared straight into the night, above the dark wall of the Horse Heaven Hills on the other side of the valley.

"Been a strange of a couple of days. That's all I got to say," he said.

Adah appeared not to hear. "Maybe it ain't that God's so big," she said. "The scientists, they say no matter how close they look or how hard they figure, they can't quite get back to that time when it all began. There's just an instant, a tiny, little speck a' time they can't see through. And the closer they look, the narrower that speck gets, but it don't go away. Maybe that's where God's been all this time. Time and space don't mean nothin' in heaven anyway. If eternity down here is an instant in God's mind, then why can't that tiny, little speck of time the scientists can't see through, that instant, be eternity to God?"

"I don't think about things like that much."

"No, son, I don't expect you do. But this here world wasn't made as a joke, or for anyone's amusement. God was deadly serious when he made the heaven and the earth. Yes sir, it's a puzzle, but those scientists ain't never going to get to the bottom of it. God understands, and we will too, but not while we're here in it, not for our own tiny little speck a time. That'll all come later."

"Seems like my dad's been gone for a long time now. I didn't know for sure where he'd gone until today, and now I just don't know anything. I was barely twelve when he left, and I been eighteen for a while. The time seemed to go by fast, but it still feels like a long time ago that he left. We been all right, Mom and me. But I wonder what it would a' been like, what I would a' been like, if he hadn't been gone."

Adah continued to stare straight ahead. The starry night sky was bright and moonless and seemed to curve down to the very spot where she stood with Grady. The lights of the house spilled a soft shadow into the empty desert in front of them. In the far distance, the stars stopped at the distinct ridgeline of the Horse

Heaven Hills. Grady shivered. He felt alone and calm and, for just an instant, still.

"But ma'am…?"

"Yes, son?"

"My dad's been in prison all this time. He ain't just been away like I thought. I found out about it today while I was in town with John."

"I know."

"Did John say anything? I wish he hadn't."

Adah didn't answer.

He continued, "I have a right to know about my father. Why'd my mom lie to me?"

"She didn't, but that ain't the point. Down here in the world, sometimes it seems like a thing matters more'n your own life. Matters so much it hurts. Hurts so much it seems like you can't think of nothin' else. But there's a little spot deep inside of you where it really don't matter. Your daddy's gone, yes sir. Left a hole. But there's a little spot, 'bout the same size as that speck a' time out in space the scientists can't see through. That little speck inside a' you is all that matters for now. All that'll ever matter really. Sooner you learn that the better."

Grady leaned back again and stretched his shoulders and neck. He looked away, above the Horse Heaven Hills. Silent tears that Adah could not see cascaded down his face in the dark.

"There ain't nothin' there. I feel all closed up inside."

"You ain't closed up, son. Not all the way. That spot won't never close up all the way. Someday it'll get filled up bigger 'n and fuller'n anything you ever saw. I know that."

"But when?"

"In God's own time, son. In God's own time."

CHAPTER 7

"Mom?" Jill asked.

"How'd your clothes get so wet?"

"Uhhh…"

"Never mind. I've got a surprise. I think we need a change."

"A change? Mom?"

Jill's mother, Anne, was dressed and had toast on the table when the girl stumbled out of her room and down the narrow hall into the kitchen.

"Eat something."

She was sorting through Jill's wet clothes. The dampness from the river had settled, but they hadn't dried out much overnight.

"How did your clothes get so wet?"

"I went out last night. It was raining when I came in. Mom, what do you mean, 'we need a change'?"

Anne dropped the clothes on the floor where she'd found them. "I haven't been much help to you since your dad died. Well…I have an aunt or great aunt or something. She's not really an aunt, more like a grandmother. I think she was my mom's aunt. I hadn't seen her since I was younger than you, then she showed up at your dad's funeral."

"Yeah? What's that got to do with me?"

"Well, she called me on the phone yesterday, before you got home from school. I guess I was asleep when you got home, or I would have told you then. But anyway, she's with an old guy who lives out in the country. Somehow, she knew things hadn't been going too well since."

"What are you trying to say?"

"She's invited us to come out and stay with her and this man. I guess she's married to him. She said sometimes a change is what people need when they are trying to get along. That's the way she put it, 'tryin' to get along.' I think she may be right. We've got no reason to stay here in this house. Every day's been the same since…"

"I've got school. Where does she live? We can't live in the country. What do people do there?"

Anne continued, "She lives on the other side of Benton City. They have a huge place, a ranch, cows, horses, a barn. All that kind of stuff. Their property goes all the way down to the Yakima River. It'll be different, a change. Maybe we'd start to see things clearer. I don't know."

"There's no one out there but hicks and rednecks! Look at me. Look at you. Do you think we belong out in the sticks with a bunch of cows? No way, Mom!"

She finished sorting the wet clothes and sat down in a chair next to her daughter at the small kitchen table. Jill was nibbling on the crust of a piece of dry toast. She was trying to think back.

"Jill?"

"Yeah?"

"When was the last time we talked about your dad?"

The question hit Jill like a punch. And, again, she felt the tug that had pulled her into the river the night before. She squeezed back the same tears and resisted the steady pull. She glanced at the pile of wet clothes on the hallway floor.

"When was it?"

"Never." The girl was quiet.

"School doesn't matter right now. I need to tell you that day hasn't gone by when I didn't think it's just too hard to go on. Every day I get up without knowing for sure whether I'll make it through to go to bed at night. I've been no mother to you at all. You've been a lot stronger than I have through all this."

Jill looked at her mother. Then she looked away. The house was warm and silent. The pile of her wet clothes sat in a lump on the hallway floor. An old car rattled by on the street. Tears spilled out of the corners of her eyes and ran in slow streaks down her cheeks.

"Mom, no. I …last night, I…"

A loud knock at the front door stopped her before she could tell her mother about her night in the river. While her mother answered the door, Jill thought about the policeman who said he might check on her.

"Ma'am?" a young cowboy said, a ratty cowboy hat in hand.

"Yes? Frank?"

"Yes, ma'am. I'm here to pick you both up. I'll take you to the ranch now. Adah says y'all should come along."

Jill would have preferred the policeman.

By noon, she and her mother were bouncing along the same dirt road that Grady had traveled in the dark the night before. In the daylight, Jill saw more of the countryside than Grady had. The Yakima turned sharply north and east at Benton City then bent even more sharply to the south ten miles farther on at Horn Rapids before it got to Richland. So, their route from town to the trailer house between Rattlesnake Ridge and the Yakima crossed the river twice. Jill thought it was the Columbia, but she wasn't sure, and she didn't ask.

She had taken half an hour to pack and pout while Frank sat impatiently in the kitchen, sipping instant coffee. Adah had said to only bring clothes. Jill had found one of her father's old sweatshirts at the bottom of a box deep in the back of her mother's bedroom closet. She put it on and pulled the oversized hood down over her forehead until it nearly covered her eyes. During the ride, she stared straight ahead as she sat between Frank and her mother for the forty-five minutes it took Frank to drive from Richland to John's place. He pulled his pickup into the driveway, and Anne, who sat on the passenger side, waited a moment before she nudged the door open with her shoulder and stepped down. Jill did not move.

Through the windshield she could see the old trailer, the barn, and the corral with the Horse Heaven Hills in the distance. She felt the tug again.

"You know there's a young guy stayin' out here too." Frank's quiet voice brought Jill's attention back to the front seat of the pickup. He had not moved from the driver's seat, and she was suddenly aware she was sitting very close to him. "They were up on the ridge gatherin' cows, and now they've gone to town. I figure you and that guy must have the same sorta trouble or Adah wouldn't a' had you all out here at the same time."

"What do you know about me?"

"Don't get worked up, girl. You didn't come out here while school is goin' on for a vacation. And John didn't ask that young feller to stay here because he needs a hand. Whenever he wants somethin' done, he just calls me, and I do it."

"I don't know what I'm doing here. And I sure don't know anything about anyone else being here. I don't even want to be here!"

"I'm none too happy with this arrangement myself, and I don't really want a' have much to do with that guy neither."

"You know him then?"

"Yeah, I do." He stopped and looked away. "I know enough not to want him here. But I figure Adah and the old man got somethin' goin' on. Somethin' they ain't going to say much about. You go on now. Git your stuff in the house. I got to go stack a truckload a hay."

Jill got out of the truck, hefted her single bag out of the back, and watched as Frank headed toward the barn where John's truck was still parked. He climbed into John's truck and started the engine. Jill took in a long, deep breath, exhaled slowly, shook her head, and followed her mother into the house.

Later when Grady and John returned from town, Jill was sitting at the table next to her mother. Adah was in her chair at the end of the table with her back to the mudroom door. She spoke softly, and the two women did not look up when Grady came in through the mudroom, paused in the doorway, and stared for a moment at Jill because she looked familiar. Grady was rubbing his knuckles when Jill glanced up. She recognized him. Immediately, she felt like she should smile or say something to him, but she remained still and said nothing.

CHAPTER 8

On the day after Grady's fight with the boys in Richland, as he had done every morning since he'd been with Adah, John rose before the sun came up. He rolled out of the warm bed, stepped into the same denim pants he had on the day before, pulled on his boots, and stood up. Before putting on a clean undershirt and a faded denim work shirt with rusty snaps, he peered through the blinds, holding the shade open an inch, so he could see what the weather was doing. This morning it was clear, and the stars glistened in the bluing morning sky. He walked around the bed and kissed Adah lightly on the forehead just as the old woman was beginning to stir awake. He was always gone from the house by the time she got up, because Adah preferred to get dressed and struggle into her chair alone while John did his pre-breakfast chores outside. He always put coffee on so Adah wouldn't have to and so he wouldn't be disappointed when he returned to the house.

Every day was the same. Predictable. Dependable.

John shrugged into his wool coat and shuffled out of the dark house and down the back steps next to Adah's ramp. Outside, the cold did not surprise him. The September air was starting to hold some of winter's dampness and chill. The fading stars and a bright light from the kitchen provided the only illumination. He stood for a moment on the back steps and gazed far across the valley. Yard lights from new houses continued to fill the dark gaps along the south side of the river. Then his eyes scanned upward to the top of the Horse Heaven Hills. No sign of clouds and no hint of wind. Soon the cold would retreat before the rising sun. It would be a warm day.

He walked down the back steps and across the yard to the barn. On the way, he opened the gate to the chicken wire kennel and released his two Aussie cow dogs. The dogs raced once around the house and sprinted headlong for the pasture.

"You go on dogs," John shouted after them with a smile. "Make sure them cows down by the river ain't got away."

He went first to the feed room at the east end of the barn. He turned on the lights and used an old coffee can scoop oats into three separate buckets from a heavy paper bag. Then he repeated the process with barley from a second bag. He carried the buckets one by one to each of his three saddle horses, who were stabled in the barn against the coming cold and threw each one a generous flake of clean alfalfa hay.

Next, he fed hay to the yearling colts in a larger stall at the other end of the barn. John kept them in the big stall with the gate open so they could get out and play in the large corral. He cleaned up four small piles of horse manure with a pitchfork and put down a fresh layer of wheat straw. While the young horses ate, John reached over the top of the gate to stroke the smooth neck of the colt nearest the fence.

"We'll let ya'll out back with the cows in a week or two," John said.

This time of year, there wasn't too much to do in the morning. Later, he would have to haul hay for the cows with the old tractor. The hay would be loaded on to a flatbed trailer every day before the sun went down, and John's early-morning chores would take longer. Finally, he fed the dogs. They ran back up from the direction of the river pasture and back into the kennel when they heard the dry dog food clatter into their metal bowl. He returned to the house and filled a thick porcelain mug with hot coffee. He went back outside and leaned his back against the corral fence to drink his coffee and watch the sun come up.

He cupped his hands around the mug and held it near his lips and waited for the dark aroma to rise. He took a short sip and felt the heat in the palms of his hands through his leather gloves and against his lips. He took the cup away from his mouth and watched the coffee ripple as he blew softly across the surface. After all this time, Grady had finally arrived. John had come to realize, in the years since the boy's father was sent to prison for killing Charlie, that his own loss and Grady's were of a single piece. John knew his son's murderer had a son of his own, and he knew the man and his young wife had sent Grady far away for a long time to save the boy from the painful attention the short trial and its aftermath would bring. John had kept careful track of Grady ever since.

Shortly after Charlie was killed, John began to pick up hitchhikers whenever he was in a rodeo town. When Grady began to rodeo, he watched the boy from a distance, careful not to make contact too soon. John had come to believe that helping Grady overcome the loss of his own father was the key to understanding all that had happened, but he needed to be certain the time was right. Adah had said something about how the present moment was often not the best time to act and to be patient and wait. But lately her strength seemed to be fading, and John did not want to meet Grady without Adah.

"Can I help?" Grady's voice startled John.

"Nope. I'm about done. Just thinkin' a little."

"John, my mom's gone to see my dad. She didn't say anything about comin' back very soon. Do you know anything? Yesterday you made it seem like you knew what's goin' on."

"I don't know nothin' about your momma. But I know a little about your daddy. I never knew him much at all, but I know about him. Where he's been. Why he's been there."

"Tell me then. What's goin' on? Mom always made it sound like he just up and ran away, packed his riggin' one morning, drove down the road, and never came back. That never seemed quite right to me."

"There's some truth in that, I reckon, but not the whole truth."

Grady slapped his hand on the corral fence. "You're speakin' in riddles, you and that old woman both. What do you know about my father?"

His fists started to clench. John walked toward the boy, removing his gloves. "I'll tell you what," he said quietly. "Your mom's likely to be back pretty soon now, and she'll be the one to tell you all this, at least all you don't find out before then."

Grady remained tense, but he had tamped the anger back down into the same deep hole. Fists still clenched, he forced his fingers apart. Calmly and quietly, he said, "I want to hear it, John. Say it out loud."

John looked at him. "Your father killed my son. We both know it. Now it's said, and we can get on with it."

Grady's shoulders relaxed, and for the moment, his anger dissipated at seeing the hurt in the old man's eyes. John softened his facial expression. He cleared his throat.

"With your momma gone, you'll want a place to stay for a while. You can stay here. I could use some help with the place, and you'll need a base to rodeo from, I 'spect. Adah's got a couple of people stayin' here too, but there's plenty of room. I ain't going to pay you, but you can help me out around the place to pay for your bed and food."

John didn't wait for a reply. He brushed past the boy and strode toward the house. Grady leaned his forearms on the top rail of the fence. The old man hadn't given him a choice. He simply told Grady how things would be. He seemed to know Grady would not turn down the offer. What other choice did he have? Go back to the empty house in Richland? He shrugged and followed John into the house.

CHAPTER 9

The morning after Jill and Anne arrived at the ranch, Adah sat on the edge of the bed and shrugged the old nightgown off over the top of her head. Her clothes had been stacked neatly on her wheelchair the night before. She pulled on an old tee shirt and a heavy woolen sweater and struggled into the loose-fitting denim pants she'd worn several days in a row. She had to pull each foot up to rest on the opposite knee to get her socks and short leather boots on. John had rolled her chair close to the bed before he went out. Adah pulled the chair closer yet, locked the wheels and hefted herself into it. The effort winded her and caused a deep gripping sensation in her chest. She sat quietly while she caught her breath.

"Not much longer," she said. "Got to be ready."

She wheeled her chair to a small desk placed so she could look out the only window in the room. After struggling a little to raise the blinds with a long cord, she could see the barn, the corral, and the long pasture that sloped off in the direction of the Yakima River. She took a very old, cloth-bound Bible from the desk and let it fall open. She began to read aloud at the top of the left-hand page.

"Hmmm …John 18:19: 'Then the high priests questioned Jesus about his disciples and about his teaching. Jesus answered, 'I have spoken openly to the world; I have always taught in the synagogues and the temples where all come together. I have said nothing in secret. Why do you ask me? Ask those who heard what I said to them; they know what I said.'"

Adah thought for a moment. *The truth is what he said. And they knew what it was. But nothing was said in secret. All this is to be made known. Listen. Wait for everything to be made known. Say nothing for now.*

Adah continued to stare out the window at the ancient rise of the Horse Heaven Hills. *Those hills ain't changed for 12,000 years, and they ain't goin' to change. Don't matter what we do.* With her eyes, she followed the recently cut gravel road that began off to the east and sliced its way to the top of the hills directly south of the ranch house. *We can scar the countryside, but we can't cut deep enough to get at the heart.*

"By and by," she said aloud. "In the sweet by and by."

She put the Bible down. When she turned her chair away from the desk, John was standing just outside the door in the hall. He was still wearing his thick coat and was stuffing his gloves into a deep pocket. She wheeled herself into the doorway and put out both hands. He stepped forward, took both of her hands and lifted her to her feet.

"Gonna be cold today?" she asked.

"No. It's mite chilly now, but by noon it should be warmin' up. That girl and her momma are already up. They're sittin' at the table like they're not sure what they should be doin'."

"Did you talk to the boy?"

"He knows we ain't sayin' all we could. I didn't tell him anything he don't need to know."

"Good. He'll find out on his own soon enough, but he can wait a bit." *The truth ain't goin' nowhere.*

Grady came down the hall just as Adah said, "wait a bit."

"Wait for what?" he asked.

"Winter," she said, her eyes again sparkling with mischief. "Wait for winter. I was tellin' John that it'll be plenty cold soon enough, all he has to do is wait. Y'all need to eat breakfast now. I'm running a little late, so it'll take a few minutes. Coffee'll be ready right quick, so you should wash up and go on in the kitchen."

The kitchen was warm and smelled faintly of bacon grease by the time Grady came back down the hall. John took a heavy mug from an open cupboard above the stove and handed it to Grady, who took it and held it out for John to fill. He poured strong coffee nearly to the brim of Grady's mug before he re-filled his own. Jill and her mother were standing near the table waiting. When Adah wheeled herself up to her place at the table, Anne sat down next to her. Jill remained standing but took a step forward to stand closer to her mother. John and Grady leaned against the kitchen counter and sipped their coffee.

"When do you figure to rodeo again?" John asked.

The small kitchen was crowded. Grady stole a glance at Jill who had turned away to face her mother. He knew he had seen the girl before but could not quite remember where.

The night before, when Jill and Anne arrived at John's ranch, the girl was dressed just as she'd been the night she tried to kill herself in the Columbia River, baggy shirt and jeans, and a much-too-large sweatshirt with a hood she kept pulled down over her face. She was not self-conscious about her body, but she didn't like the games that were required when a boy thought she might be attractive or available.

"Jill, honey," Adah had said at dinner the first night. "I don't give hoot nor holler about what you wear while you're out here with the white trash. But you'll not cover your face at this table. If you're goin' to sit down to eat with us, we gotta right to see what you look like while you do it."

Jill looked out from under her hood, twisted her mouth into a pout, and stared at her mother, hopeful that Anne might intervene. But Anne continued to eat and did not look at her daughter. Jill sighed and shrugged. She pulled her hood off and shook out her un-brushed hair.

"Better," Adah said. "You're not as unattractive as I thought. What do you think, Grady?" When Adah mentioned Grady's name,

Jill's faced heated up and her cheeks reddened enough to make Grady pay more attention to the food on his plate.

The next morning, when Grady saw Jill at the breakfast table without her hood, he recalled how she'd been almost always alone at school, her narrow body hidden by a heavy coat and much of her face covered with the hood. One time, a male teacher or principal, someone who enjoyed making kids do what they were told, made Jill take off her hood so he could see her face while he talked. Jill pulled her hood off and shook her hair out the same way she'd done at Adah's dinner table.

Grady's circle of non-rodeo acquaintances was small enough he thought he should be able to easily recognize anyone from outside that world. But now, on a cool September morning in the homey warmth of Adah's kitchen and with the generous aroma of a meaty breakfast filling the air, Jill seemed different from the girl he remembered. She was wearing a tee shirt with a hummingbird on the front that fit well enough to draw his attention to her small breasts. Her jeans were still baggy, but they hung a bit below where her delicate waist joined her narrow hips. When he realized she was watching him, his face reddened, and he looked away. When he looked back, he noticed her hair had been brushed and pulled back. Jill had a full face, dominated by deep-set, dark brown eyes. He watched from his spot at the counter until she turned her head and caught him. She didn't smile, but she didn't look away either.

He took another sip from the mug, set the cup down, pushed himself away from the counter, and leaned back. His back had stiffened up again after the long ride with John and his cows, and he felt the hard fall in Ellensburg in all the usual places. The one-sided fight with the boys in Richland hadn't helped.

Jill looked down at her mother and then glanced back at Grady. They locked eyes for a second and in that moment, she remembered him clearly. She hadn't exactly been attracted to him at Richland High School, but she had admired the way he seemed to move through the school day utterly unconcerned with what anyone else thought. As she watched him drink coffee in Adah's kitchen, she began to understand what it was that had impressed her at school.

Everything about Grady seemed to fit. Jill knew some kids liked to wear cowboy hats and boots, and she remembered one or two boys who would strut around school with oversized belt buckles. But those kids always seemed to be in costume. But here was Grady. He wore a cowboy hat and a big belt buckle, and the cuffs of his tight, straight-legged Wranglers bunched up at the ankle of his narrow-toed, leather cowboy boots. And everything seemed to fit. She tried but could not imagine him dressed any other way.

She noticed how the muscles rolled up under his shirt when he shrugged his shoulders. She had once been startled by his loosely tethered violence when took on three fat football players who'd tried to knock his hat off. But usually, he'd been quiet and seemed to take possession of whatever space he occupied. He was not so much a loner, as someone who simply didn't need the shallow validation of other kids. Jill liked that about him. And the finely muscled shoulders that bunched up under his shirt were nice too.

As Anne rose from her chair, she tugged on her daughter's arm so Jill would follow her out of the kitchen. They disappeared down the hall, and Grady quickly shifted his attention back to John.

"I'd like to make Pendleton in a couple of weeks. The money there is real good. I've never taken on the big rodeos much before now. The bulls at Pendleton are really good. I got to check to see if I have enough to make fees, though."

"That's the way it is, ain't it? You got to ride to make money, but you can't ride if you got no money. Don't worry about fees. I'll loan you money for fees and you can pay me back outa your winnings."

"But I may not win anything. That's not a real good bet for you, John."

"Well, I liked what I saw in Ellensburg. With a little luck you'd a' stayed on then, and we wouldn't be talkin' about your fees now."

"Well, I don't know. I kinda like to pay my way."

"Stop now," Adah spoke more sternly than Grady thought necessary. "I reckon you'll have plenty enough to be thankful for, just getting' down the road. Just say 'thank ya' and go on and ride them bulls. What's that old man need money for anyway?"

John and Grady were long gone, working on a stretch of fence below the house by the time Jill came out of the bedroom. Anne was already sitting at the table in the warm kitchen drinking coffee when her daughter came down the hall. The girl was still not quite sure where she was or what she was doing there.

After they had arrived at the ranch with Frank the day before, Adah showed them to the spare room at the end of the hall next to the smaller room where Grady had slept. They stayed in the room unpacking and settling in until Adah called them to dinner for quick introductions and a quiet meal.

Jill knew a little about Grady. They had been at Richland High School at the same time for a while. She knew there had been a fight and he'd stopped coming to school. She was also surprised Frank didn't stay to eat until she remembered he'd said something about his brother and not wanting to have anything to do with Grady.

After the meal, she returned to the room she was to share with her mother and stretched out on one of two old beds set against opposite walls with a large window between them. She stared at the ceiling, recalling the burning sensation in her lungs.

Jill's mind settled on her father, but the silent tears that usually flowed down her cheeks and dripped off her chin did not appear this time. The early evening faded fast and her mother, who was helping Adah with the dishes and talking, came to bed late. Jill was lying silently on the bed with her clothes still on when Anne came in the room.

"You ought to get dressed for bed."

"I'm fine, Mom. How long are we going to stay here?"

"I've been talking to Adah. She really is a good woman, you know. She says we can stay as long as we need to. They've got room and we can help her out a bit."

"What about school? I'd like to, maybe, you know, graduate someday."

"Jill, I think we need to change things. This isn't permanent, but if we can get things sorted out here, maybe we can both get on with our lives."

"Whatever."

"Try to sleep. We may have to get up early tomorrow."

"What does the old woman say we should do out here? What can we do here that we can't do back in Richland? You can't even see the neighbors from here. There's not another house as far as you can see. What are we supposed to do?"

"Jill, you never had much to do with the neighbors or anyone else in town. I guess we're just supposed to wait. Adah says we should take it one day at a time. And wait. Maybe then we'll know what to do."

Jill did not respond. She felt the tug again. She wanted to get up and leave the room, walk out of the house and out of her own life. She made no effort to push the tug back down, but she didn't move from the bed either.

She turned on her side, away from her mother. "I can wait here too," she said to herself. And she wondered how long the wait would be. Then she remembered what Frank had said about Grady.

∗∗∗

The second day Jill woke up late, long after John and Grady had left the house. Even though she'd brushed her hair again and left the oversized sweatshirt behind, she felt relieved when she came into the kitchen and found no one there except her mother washing the morning dishes at the sink. Adah was in her chair at the table.

"You're a mite late for breakfast, darlin'. John and Grady're already out and about, but there's bread for toast and plenty of coffee left." Adah's voice caught Jill by surprise. She was used to getting up while her mother was still asleep and having the house to herself until she left for school. Breakfast was normally a box of tiny chocolate doughnuts or a bag of chips washed down with a sixty-four-ounce Coke from the 7-Eleven on the way to school.

"I'm not hungry."

"Jill, honey, eat something, please." Anne watched Jill closely as she rinsed the dishes in the sink.

"Maybe some coffee then," the girl said. "But I really don't want anything to eat."

Anne turned away from the sink abruptly. "Jill, I'm going to take a walk."

"Take your time, honey," Adah warned. "You can get down to the river on a cow path that starts just at the gate out back by the barn. Or you can take the trail at the end of the driveway that heads up toward the ridge, the same way John and Grady went the day you and Jill come out here. You can't get lost as long as you keep the house in sight."

"Mom, wait." She did not feel like being left alone with Adah. Old people made her nervous, and she couldn't remember ever having to spend time with anyone in a wheelchair. "I'll come too."

"No, honey. You stay and talk with Adah. We're going to be here a while, so you might as well get acquainted."

Jill poured herself coffee from the pot on the stove and sat at the table. Adah pulled herself up out of her chair and stood at the sink drying the dishes Anne had washed. She leaned against the counter to take the pressure off her weak legs.

"It seems like someone ought to help you with that," Jill said, but she did not move from her place at the table.

"I manage alright. I can usually get things washed up and dried. Most times someone else has to come and put the dishes away. Some days I feel like I'm getting stronger, but I can't stay on my feet too long."

Jill sighed. *So, this is the way it's going to be*, she thought. *I'm going to be a maid for this old bag, and my mother thinks she's helping us. Right.*

"There," Adah said. She placed the last of the dishes in the drying rack. "I reckon we can let them air out a bit today.

"So, Jill, tell me what you think of our place out here."

She was surprised. She hadn't really thought much about the place at all.

"I don't know," she said. "I mean it's a place, I guess. There aren't many people around."

"No, and that's a fact. It's a good long ways to the west before you get to any neighbors. About two miles, I guess. Folks over yonder got a hay field in. Doin' pretty good I hear. You go down the hill to the south and it's about two miles to the river. It's nice down there. Maybe you can get Frank or someone to take you down that-a-way. It's a good long walk or you could ride one of John's horses."

"I don't think I'll be riding any horses. There's not much to do out here, so I guess I'll just do my time until Mom decides we can go back to Richland."

"I see. Well, if you was to go off to the east, it's about three, no three and half miles to the Hanford Highway, which was called Horne Road in the old days, and runs through Benton City off in one direction and all the way to Hanford along the river in the other. John's land ends about a mile and a half over that-a-way. There's a good fence that runs along the line from the river all the way up toward the ridgeline 'til you get to the nuclear reservation boundary.

"That'd be off to the north and east, I guess. Nothin' that way. No people and just that big ol' government fence to keep John's cows from gettin' into somethin' that might make 'em glow in the dark."

The thought of cows glowing in the dark caused Jill to smile against her will. Adah did not miss it.

"I reckon you'll be alright out here. I been talkin' to your momma, and you and her got a lot of time to make up. Your daddy…"

"I don't know what she told you, but I'm fine with that."

Jill felt the tug again. She thought of the river. She didn't know which river it was, just two miles away and down the hill.

"I mean I miss him and all, but I wish Mom would mind her own business. I'm fine."

Adah sat carefully in her chair, reached down with her left hand to release the brake and wheeled herself to the table. Jill squeezed her hands into two clenched fists on the table in front of her and turned away. The sudden tears welling in her eyes surprised her. She squeezed the tears back down before she had to wipe them off her cheeks.

"I'm sure you're handlin' things fine, darlin." Adah put her hand on the girl's fists. The warmth in Adah's wrinkled fingers surprised Jill. "But I think maybe your momma might need some help. She's hurtin', and maybe you can ease her pain some."

Still looking away from Adah, she let the tears flow. She turned and faced the old woman, and her lower jaw began to tremble.

As she pulled her fists away, she replied, "I said, I'm just fine. My mother will have to deal with the fact that I'm just fine. If she…if you…want to rescue someone, you'll both have to look for someone else."

She stood up quickly and turned to leave. Adah's hand caught the girl's arm, and Jill's shock at the force of the old woman's grip paralyzed her for a moment.

"You listen, child!"

She tried once to pull away, but Adah pulled her back down.

"Now listen. You got to wait for things to happen. And things will happen when they're a' mind to. You been brought out here by your momma, but there's more. You'll see. This place ain't no place special, but it's a place you can rest and where you can wait. A place where your momma, and maybe you too, can rescue whoever needs to be rescued. Do you hear me, girl?"

She listened desperately for some familiar sound, traffic, wind through the trees, a fragment of song from the radio, the air conditioner, anything. But she could discern nothing except a dense, alien silence and the pressure of the old woman's determined grip on her arm.

"I don't know if I can."

"It's quiet here, and you got a lot racin' around in your head. You can hear a good deal more than you think."

She stood up slowly. Adah did not stop her. She walked out of the kitchen and down the hall to the small bed in the neat room. She buried her face and pounded both fists into the pillow and screamed.

***

John often did not sleep through the night. At such times he busied himself with small jobs, usually in the barn or the tack room. And he brooded over the fate of his sons. Robert, his middle son, had moved to Idaho. John had not heard from him in more than five years. Frank was usually close by, but he was disappearing more and more often into a fog of alcohol and depression. Charlie was dead. After a sleepless night, the sunrise always found John in a foul mood.

The next morning, Grady woke up very early. He lay on his back in the dark room and did not move. He sat up, pulled his feet out from under the blankets, and slung both legs over the edge of the bed and onto the floor. He stood up and shuffled to the window that looked north across the narrow yard and then into the solid black mass of Rattlesnake Ridge. When he parted the thin curtain, he could see an ocean of starlight above the ridge.

He sat back on the bed and was surprised by the faint sound of someone moving about at the other end of the house. He quickly took his Wranglers from a chair near the door and put them on. He sat back down and found his boots under the edge of the bed. The leather was stiff in the morning, especially if the house was cold, and he had to bend his back and grunt to pull on each boot. The right boot was easy, but he had to stand on the left and pull up with both arms and push down hard with his left leg before his heel snapped into place. He bounced lightly on both legs so his feet would settle in. He left the room quickly and was still buttoning his shirt when he met John coming down the hall from the opposite direction.

"You're up early," John said. He turned aside so Grady could pass then continued down the hall toward the bedroom where Grady assumed Adah was still sleeping.

"Coffee's made in the kitchen. I'll be there directly."

"Sure, I'll meet you in the kitchen, I guess."

Grady took two tentative backward steps, then turned and headed to the kitchen. A pale light spilled out from the far end of the dim hallway. He smelled fresh coffee even before he left his room, and when he turned the corner at the end of the hall, the kitchen was filled with the familiar, brown, early-morning aroma. His father drank "cowboy" coffee, strong enough to keep him going until lunch and thick enough to eat with a spoon, or at least that was the way his mother described her husband's acrid morning brew.

Grady could see John's heavy mug filled with coffee sitting on the counter. He took a similar mug from the cupboard and carefully poured some for himself. He cupped the mug in both hands, took a careful sip, and waited for the quiet buzz, which was the object of the morning's first cup. *It's not as strong as my father's coffee*, Grady thought, *but it ain't bad.*

He leaned back against the counter, took two more careful sips, and watched the steam rise from the mug while he waited for John to return. He held his mug close to his face so the aroma would waft up with the steam. He liked the comforting feel of heat radiating into his palms. He continued to sip slowly, taking in a little more each time as the coffee cooled. Leaning against the counter in the snug kitchen with the coffee sitting warmly in his stomach, Grady thought about Jill.

At school kids like Jill seemed to want no one to know anything about them. They were either deliberately angry or genuinely depressed and almost always alone. Grady strutted through the crowds at school. He wore his arrogance like a badge of honor, and his aloof nature was a challenge to other boys who saw it as their duty to make sure the cocky cowboy was put in his place. Grady never backed down, so their attempts to restore their view of the proper order usually ended badly. Jill and the handful of other girls like her were aggressive only in their efforts to remain invisible. But on the ranch, with her baggy clothes and hood removed, he was beginning to see something more than sadness or anger in Jill. *Why'd she come out here*, he kept asking himself. Then, *but I'm kinda glad she did.* His mug was half empty by the time he heard John coming down the hall.

"So, you think you want to get to Pendleton?" John said. "About a week from now?" His tone was abrupt and caused Grady to tense up. He saw that John was staring at him, so he waited a few seconds and lowered his mug before answering.

"Yeah. That's been the plan. I did pretty good at Kennewick last month. Almost won a check the day you picked me up in Ellensburg. So, I guess Pendleton is the next step."

"You reckon you'll need to beat anyone half to death while you're down there?" John looked away then set his jaw and turned his back to Grady.

"I …What is it you want me to say, John?"

"Why'd you beat on that kid in Richland? He mighta been a pissant, but him and his friends wasn't going to do much. It didn't matter to me none. They'd a' got bored and went on their way if you'd stayed out of it."

Grady put the mug down and slowly closed his fists with his hands at his side. He felt the skin tighten as it stretched over his swollen knuckles, and tension ran up his arms and caused him to shrug and roll his shoulders. His chest felt tight, and his breathing became shallow.

"They was kids actin' like punks. Like them two boys at the Conoco. I can't stand to see people behave like that, so I…"

"So, you do that boy in town the same way?"

"Why're you bringin' this up now? What do you want me to do about it now? I know I shouldn't a' beat that kid so bad, but I…"

John remained silent. He turned his back on Grady and looked out the window. The eastern sky had begun to brighten, but it was still fully dark outside. Grady did not move.

"I don't believe you should ride any more bulls for a while," John said without turning around. "You need to get your mind right. You got to get this thing about your daddy straight."

"Dammit, John! If you know somethin' about my dad, tell me. If you don't, leave it be."

John turned away from the window and faced Grady. His voice remained calm and steady, with no anger in it.

"My boy was killed in a fight. You know that. Do you understand? All my boys is gone now, one way or another. We ain't been the same. It ain't goin' to be the same."

"I'm askin' again, John," he said. "Why'd you bring me here? What am I doing here with you and that old woman? What do you want from me?"

John put his hands on the boy's shoulders, held them there for a moment, and then gently pushed the boy away.

"I don't know, son. Seemed like the right thing to do."

Grady leaned back against the counter again. Adah wheeled her chair into the kitchen, stopped between them, and set the brake. Outside the sun was peaking over the eastern horizon, and the darkness that had enveloped the house and the countryside began to melt away. She started to stand up, but after one feeble effort, decided to remain seated.

"Now what's all this?" she said. "Got kinda loud out here for a minute."

"Adah," Grady said. "I want to know what you all know about my dad. Why am I here? Why's that girl here?"

John absently drained off the last of his coffee and held the empty mug at his side with a single finger hooked through the handle.

"Grady, we only know what you know," Adah said. "Now, I reckon you got up before dawn 'cause you got work to do, so you best get started. I'll call you for breakfast when it's ready."

"No!" he said. "This is bullcrap!" He jammed his hat down onto his head and stormed through the mudroom and out the back door, heading for the corral.

"Yes, son. It is," she said. "Most things is."

John had not moved.

"Well, old man. You got anything to say?"

"No," he said. "I 'spect I've said about enough."

She rolled her chair to him and reached out and put her hand on his forearm as the mug continued to dangle at the end of his index finger.

"Well, John. That ain't no bullcrap."

CHAPTER 10

Jill was already awake when she heard Grady in the kitchen. Her mother was still asleep in the other bed. *Moving out to the country hadn't changed Mom's sleep patterns much*, Jill thought. She heard the back door slam and then waited for several minutes before she got up and dressed quickly. She put on her heavy sweatshirt but left the hood hanging loosely from her shoulders. She checked to make sure no one was in the hall then went into the small bathroom and closed the door. She brushed her hair in front of the mirror, making sure for the first time that her face was fully visible. She wished she had some makeup with her but shook her head when she realized makeup wouldn't matter much to Grady. The realization surprised her. *Why do I even care what he thinks?*

By the time she finished in the bathroom and went into the kitchen, Grady was gone. And John was headed outside through the mudroom door.

Adah stood at the stove with her chair pushed out of the way. She was stirring something yellow in the huge cast iron frying pan. Jill assumed it was eggs scrambled with some kind of salty meat. The spicy smell of the meat cooking with the eggs and the bracing aroma of coffee brewing reminded Jill of where she was. She had no recollection of any particular smell connected with breakfast at home. She had no recollection of breakfast at all.

"Mornin', girl," Adah said. "Breakfast will be ready in a little bit. You and me can sit down with the men folk when it's ready."

"Men folk? Grady? He seems more like a boy to me. He's not much older than I am. Besides, I heard him yelling at John this morning."

"Well, John wasn't quite himself. I reckon he'll make peace with Grady. I'm not sure what Grady will do. It's easier for an old man 'cause he ain't got so much to lose."

Adah stopped stirring. She used two hands and a heavy potholder to lift the pan off the stove. She turned and handed the pan to Jill.

"Here you go, put this on that block a wood on the table. Then get yourself some coffee. There's biscuits about ready. When they're done, your mom'll be up, and we can all eat."

Jill took the frying pan from Adah and placed it on the table. She took the last of the heavy mugs from the cupboard and filled it with coffee. She tried to take a sip, but the coffee was too hot to drink. She glanced out the kitchen window and saw Grady putting two large plastic buckets away in the tack room at the east end of the barn.

"Maybe I'll go tell John and Grady that breakfast is about ready," Jill said.

"Don't be long, girl. Biscuits'll be ready in few minutes," Adah said. After Jill had gone, she whispered to herself, "You take as much time as you need." She moved to the window where she could see the corral. Grady was leaning with his forearms on the top rail of the fence. Jill approached but stopped about ten feet behind him.

"I thought you had work to do out here," she said.

He turned toward her and leaned back against the corral fence.

"Somebody's got to hold this fence up," he said.

Two colts came out of the barn into the corral. The first was a leggy bay who pranced over to the fence and rested his chin on the top rail where Grady was standing. The other young horse shied away cautiously to the other side of the corral. Jill approached the bay and reached her hand out, but she wasn't close enough to touch him. The colt pressed against the fence and extended his nose far enough for Jill to reach with her fingertips. She touched the colt's nose and quickly pulled her hand away. The colt reacted by pulling his head back and leaning away from the fence. Jill took a step back, and the colt returned to the fence.

"You can pet 'im," Grady said. "That sorrel filly over there is pretty shy, but this little guy likes people."

She moved carefully toward the fence, and the bay colt reached his nose toward her again.

"Will he bite me?"

"Nah. He's a pretty nice boy."

She stepped up close enough to reach the colt's forehead. Grady turned and stood next to her. He reached out and gently stroked the colt's face.

"Look," he said. "Just reach up real slow and stroke the side of his face."

Grady edged over closer to her, took her hand, and placed her fingers on the colt's face. The young horse turned his body slightly, and Grady took his hand away and told Jill to run her closed fist slowly down the line of muscle where the colt's neck and shoulder met.

"My dad told me if you pet a nervous horse like that, they'll calm right down 'cause that's how their momma nuzzled 'em when they was babies."

The colt's body was parallel to the fence now, so she could reach easily between the top two rails and pet his shoulder. "Why doesn't the other horse come over here?" she asked. "Doesn't he like to be petted?"

"She's a filly. A girl," he said. "She's shy, doesn't completely trust people yet."

"Maybe she just likes being left alone." Jill turned sideways and leaned her shoulder against the fence, so she was facing Grady, who remained with his back to the corral.

He turned his head and looked at her. She seemed taller, as she watched the filly on the other side of the corral. He turned again to face her.

"What are you and your mom doin' out here?"

"I don't know. Mom seems to think we need a change. But I don't think anything changes."

"I knew you back at Richland High," he said. "I mean, I knew about you. You never seemed like you wanted anyone to know you. You always sat by yourself, in a corner of the cafeteria or on the stairs way off where no one else ever went."

"If I didn't, there were always girls who'd make fun of me. I didn't care what they thought. I just wanted to be left alone."

"So," he said again. "What are you doin' out here?"

Adah came to the back door in her chair. "Breakfast's getting' cold. Y'all come on in now."

Jill reached out and stroked the bay colt's neck one more time then headed for the house. She stopped after two or three steps and turned around to face Grady who was still leaning on the fence.

"I don't know. What *are* we *doin'* out here?" she said.

She turned and went into the house.

✶✶✶

Later Jill leaned against the back of the house and watched Grady towel off near the tack room door. She didn't care for boys she saw at school, who had cultivated their yellowish tans with weeks of lying in the sun on the banks of the river or hours baking in a tanning salon. Grady's skin was not tanned. It was an honest, irresistible brown. He wiped the sweat off his face and then off his arms and shoulders with his tee shirt. The long muscles on both sides of his spine stretched out and bulged against the dark skin of his back and the thin denim of his worn Wranglers tightened across his buttocks and down his thick thighs when he bent over to wipe hay dust off his boots. Jill unconsciously covered her mouth and giggled when she realized both hands were trembling. He was still bent over, rubbing his lower back, when she approached.

"Smelly work today," she said.

"Yeah. Frank brought in another load of hay, but he won't work with me. I had to put it up in the barn by myself."

"That seems like a lotta trouble for cows."

"Cows got to eat. My dad told me things got to get done even when it's trouble to do 'em. Sometimes things need doin'."

"John said you got in 'some trouble' in Richland," she said. "Was beating that cowboy up something your dad would say 'needed doin'?"

He stared at her but said nothing. She stared back until he dropped his eyes.

"I think I might ride down and check on those cows by the river," he said. "It's a short ride. Do you want to come along?"

His question surprised Jill. "I've never been on a horse. I don't think I can do that. It doesn't sound very safe."

"Nah. You weren't much scared of that colt this morning. We'll take John's good horses. All you'll have to do is sit there and let the horse take care of you."

An hour later, they were riding John's horses down the mile-and-a-half long slope from John's place to the Yakima River to check on the cattle. The cows and their calves had moved down the hill in search of greener grass and the certainty of good water near the river. The early afternoon sun had dried the September chill out of the air. It would be a hot afternoon. Jill was grateful for the warmth. She'd left her oversized sweatshirt at the house. She wore only a tee shirt tucked into her jeans. She wished she had a shirt like some of the girls wore at school, one size too small.

He led the way, but he kept looking back toward her. The girl had one hand gripped tightly on the saddle horn and was leaning back on the reins. He stopped his horse to let her catch up. Her horse stopped by herself when she reached Grady.

"I'm not much of a horseman," he said. "But I know that old girl ain't gonna hurt you. Just sit up nice and easy and don't pull on the reins more'n you need to. You can hold onto the saddle horn, but only for balance."

"I'm scared," she said.

"Everyone is at first." He remembered a time when he was little, and his father had swept him up and onto the bare back of an old rope horse. He remembered his father's words.

"You got to trust the horse," he told her. "She's been down the road. Just let her do her job." She was still scared, but she relaxed a little, and after a short time, she felt her body begin to move with the rhythm of the horse's gentle gait.

They rode slowly and took nearly an hour to reach the river. Grady dismounted, and when he helped Jill down from her horse, the girl felt tenderness trickle into the same dark spot where the cold tug had been located. As he helped her dismount, she let his hands slide along each side of her body and very close to her small breasts. They left the horses to graze on the soft grass that grew at the edge of the water. Grady and Jill stood on the riverbank and stared at the free-flowing Yakima River.

"There's a lot of water here," she said. "And it's moving so fast." She sat down on a flat stone, and he sat beside her on the ground with his legs stretched out in front of him. He rubbed his thighs with the heels of his hands, trying to force the stiffness and pain out of his muscles. His knuckles were swollen, and the jagged cut on the ring finger of his right hand had not closed up all the way.

"Do your legs hurt?" she asked.

"Some."

"Then why do you do it?"

"Do what?"

"Why do you ride bulls? It seems like a lot a' risk for not much money."

"I know how. It's what I learned from my dad when I was little and from other guys later on."

She continued to stare at the water. She felt the tug once again but was able to push it back down without difficulty. Slow tears began to trickle down her cheeks, but she did not cry.

"What is it?" he asked. "What's wrong?"

"My dad died when I was fourteen. A car crash. I was in the car with him. I almost died too. Sometimes I wish I would have."

He leaned back on his arms and moved closer to her.

"I'm sorry. I didn't know what happened exactly. My dad's in prison. I just found out for sure the day after I came out here to John's place. I thought he got out after a little while and just run off. At least that's what my mom told me, or what she let me believe. I don't know which. Runnin' off didn't seem like him at all, but it was easy to believe he was too ashamed to come home when he got out."

Her tears stopped abruptly, but she didn't dry her eyes. She turned toward him and slid off the flat stone and came to rest on her knees next to him.

"John and Adah know something, but they won't say what it is. Now my mom's gone off somewhere and I don't know what's next."

She recalled the rainy night on the damp park bench. She remembered the streetlight from beneath the surface of the Columbia River. She felt herself drawn toward the water again, but the tug felt different.

"Maybe the cold water would help your legs."

She stood up and helped him to his feet. He pulled off his boots and his socks and helped Jill pull hers off. They walked side by side to the river. He stepped into the stiff current, but she stopped and watched the water rush by. She stepped into the river a few feet upstream from him, and they waded together, away from the bank. The water rose quickly to their knees and soaked through their jeans. Then after one more careful step, the river swept Jill's feet away. Grady reached with his right hand to catch her, and the cold water stung sharply where his hand had been cut. Then the pain in his swollen knuckles began to ease, just as Jill regained her footing.

She put her arms around him and settled her cheek into the space between his neck and shoulder. Grady did not move for a time. Then he put his arms around her and held her close as they drifted away from the shore. They let the river take them, and the current rolled them over until they were fully submerged and sliding along the sandy bottom. The water was not running as high as it had been during the near flood three weeks earlier and was clear enough so that Jill could see the sun from beneath the surface. When they emerged a few yards downstream, the frigid flow of the Yakima had washed away the ache.

Back onshore they lay down next to each other in the prairie grass, while the afternoon waned, and the high desert sun dried their clothes and warmed away the numbness. Grady lay very still with his hands at his sides, but he thought about pulling Jill toward him and taking her in his arms. He felt the sun warm on his bare chest, and he could feel the muscles in his shoulders and legs begin to relax. Then he felt her hand against his cheek. She sat up and removed her wet tee shirt. He ached with desire as he turned toward her, and she nestled in next to him with her head on his shoulder. She reached across his body and pulled herself even closer.

There was no sound except the progress of the river. The familiar world of grief and uncertainty retreated, so that Jill and Grady were aware of nothing but the faint pungency of sage brush and the fecund muskiness of the riverside combined with the heat of the prairie sun and warmth of skin.

They did not move for a long time. She leaned over and kissed him softly on the lips. He felt as if he had been absorbed by the warm sand. She pulled her head back, and he opened his eyes.

"Will you take me away from here?" she said. "Just for a while?"

His mind went blank. She put her hand on his cheek and pulled his attention back to her.

"Yeah," he said. "We should go."

It was late in the afternoon when they rose together and rode slowly back home.

***

The sun had begun to settle toward the horizon by the time Grady and Jill were back at John's place. He put the horses away while she leaned against the corral fence where she could watch. He put a rope halter on her horse and tied the mare to a fence post. Then he walked the old sorrel gelding he'd ridden into the corral. The horse stood calmly while he unbuckled the rear cinch and pulled the knot out of the nylon latigo, which secured the saddle in front. He reached under the horse and unsnapped the breast collar before unbuckling the left side and letting the leather strap fall away to dangle from the saddle on the right side. The horse did not move.

"Done this before, haven't you? Some people just know how to act," he said.

He walked around the rear of the horse, pulled the flank cinch, the latigo, and the breast collar together and tossed them gently over the horse's back onto the saddle seat. The old gelding still did not move. Grady walked around the rear of the horse to the left side again, grabbed the saddle pad at each end and lifted the pad and the saddle off the horse at the same time. The gelding stood and waited while Grady lifted the entire rig onto the top rail of the corral fence.

He returned to the horse, unbuckled the throatlatch, pulled the headstall over his ears, and let the horse spit the bit out. With the bit removed, the gelding strolled away from Grady and immediately began to circle and sniff the ground. He knew the horse was looking for a place to drop and roll. Grady hung the bridal on the saddle horn and repeated the process with Jill's horse.

"My father is gone. He's not coming back. At least you know where yours is."

"Yeah, I know exactly where he is. But he's still gone."

"Maybe it's the same. I think Adah would say it's the same."

"No, I reckon it ain't. But your mom…she's trying to come back. Ain't she?" he said.

"My mom's as dead to me as my father."

"But she's comin' back. She ain't, like you said, dead to you."

"Can a person come back from the dead?" she asked.

He stared off into the distance toward the Horse Heaven Hills. Then he climbed out of the corral and stood behind her.

"I reckon they can. I 'spect we may be seein' it."

"If my mom can come back, then your dad'll come back."

"He said he would. Maybe things ain't got bad enough yet. Mom's heard from him. Maybe I will too. If he don't come back, I guess I'll have to go to him."

"But my dad is never coming back." Her eyes filled again, and a single, slow tear wandered down each cheek, but she did not feel the tug. In its place was a warm feeling, not as strong as the cold tug, but no less insistent. Grady reached around her and touched her hand.

"I don't know, Jill. Seems like I ain't sure of much but bulls. But I'm here. I'm here for now. I can't say much about later on, only for now."

She turned to face him and lifted her eyes. He wiped away one tear then the next with the swollen knuckle of his right index finger. The sunlight angled in low and filtered through the dust of the corral where the two saddle horses lounged. Jill thought of her father and buried her face in Grady's shoulder and cried hard. He stroked her hair and let his hand stop at the nape of her neck. She looked up at him.

"You're here? For now?"

The gray haze of the corral dust surrounded them. They did not speak for a long time.

"For now is good," she said finally. "Better than never."

✶✶✶

The eastern sky was beginning to darken, and a deep blue had begun to follow the setting sun into the western distance by the time Jill and Grady returned to the house. Adah had another big meal ready. During dinner Anne sat stunned as her daughter devoured a half dozen ribs and a small mountain of mashed potatoes drenched in spicy, white gravy. John and Grady ate then left the house through the mudroom.

"Jill," she said. "I can't remember the last time I've seen you eat like this. What did you and Grady *do* down at that river?"

"Nothing much. We talked."

"What could you have talked about all that time?"

Jill did not answer.

Anne let it go and started to clean up the dinner dishes. Jill was still at the table, cleaning up the last of the gravy on her plate with a thick piece of Adah's bread.

"Jill, honey," Adah said. "Come out back and sit with me a spell."

Without comment, she wolfed down the last of her gravy-soaked bread and got up from the table to follow Adah's chair out the back door.

***

"Sit down here, child," Adah said, motioning Jill to a green spot on the dry grass behind the house. Adah waited for her to get settled. Then she began.

"My mother couldn't read much, but she used to tell me stories about this place."

She took a deep breath and sat back in her chair. The autumn sun had dipped toward its daily demise in the west, and the shadows were growing longer. Jill sat on the grass in front of Adah. The girl pulled her knees to her chest and stared at the darkening slope of the Horse Heaven Hills. She thought of her father. She almost told Adah what little she remembered about the night he died. She opened her mouth to speak but paused and pushed the words back down. Jill was beginning to understand she couldn't hold the past back much longer. Her own story kept rising up from that same deep, dark spot.

"I never thought of stories being about a place," she said. "I always thought stories were about people."

"Look out there on that slope, just above where the far riverbank begins," Adah said. She pointed vaguely to the south. "My family's story would've been plenty different in another place, different if we lived here today instead of back then. The years change the surface of a place, the same way they change people. But change ain't always for the best.

"I reckon I even tell the stories different now than when they was happenin'. I been around so long, I 'spect I know those old stories even better'n I know what happened just yesterday."

"But you must have forgotten some things? No offense, Adah, but it's been a long time."

"Honey, it has been a long time. But I've lived enough to know what a youngun' like you might need from those stories. You see, no one tells a story 'cept to give a bit of it to someone else. Your own story, 'bout what happened to your daddy and what you ain't been doin' about it, well, that story belongs to you and it ain't been told. But if you was to tell it to someone else, to tell all of it to someone else…"

"Grady?"

"I don't know for sure. Maybe. The thing is, our stories is not some little part of us that don't matter. They're all of what we are whether we tell 'em or write 'em down or whether we don't. They're just like our own lives 'cause they're true. But even the truth don't do no good until we give it up."

"Grady hasn't given up much. I know his father's been in jail, and I know if John hadn't been there, he might have killed that boy in Richland. That's not much of a story. And my mom, she won't say anything," Jill said.

"That boy's making it up as he goes along. He ain't got no real story of his own, not one he knows for sure. And your momma, I don't think she quite knows what you need to hear, what you need to know from her. You got to remember your momma and your daddy was together a long time before you came along. Your momma's lost ever'thing, child. Your daddy…and you."

Adah stopped. She folded her hands and placed them prayerfully in her lap.

The breeze, which still carried a premonition of winter's chill, had subsided. Jill put her hands on the grass behind her and stared at the stars blinking on one by one directly above the hills across the valley. As dusk faded, she smelled the sage outside the yard. The far-off rush of the Yakima River was an indistinct whisper, and she remembered again the night she nearly drowned in the slow water of the Columbia. She closed her eyes and thought of herself in the Yakima with Grady, his strong arms as he held her while they were submerged, how he lifted her above his head when they returned to the surface, how easy it had been to stay alive and how pleasant not to struggle. She thought of how the cold water drenched her thin tee shirt, revealing to Grady the subtle curves of her young woman's body. Her mind fixed on the long, weightless moment when he held her over his head. She remembered the brief thrill as he began to lower her back into the water, and his hands slid easily upward from her waist toward her breasts. When her feet reached the rocky river bottom, Grady paused, and without turning her away, pushed her gently toward the bank.

The breeze returned briefly, but from the southwest and without a hint of winter.

"Adah, nothing out here is like what I'm used to. At home there's only school and people who can't see anything much beyond the next day."

"Look yonder," Adah said. "There's nothin' much between you and me and the sky above them hills. Child, you got a story to share that might make that boy's way easier, might make your momma's way easier, might even make your own way easier. You're carrying a lot of hurt. But maybe you're able to carry just a little more. Might ease Grady's angry load some. Might let him ease off his own self."

"I don't get it. I don't understand."

"Grace."

"Grace?"

"Honey, you all think you got to see what's comin'. I don't know what's comin'. I only know what's passed by. I don't know what you and that boy have to say to each other. But it seems to me that you're both here. Listen, girl, I don't much believe in accidents."

The evening breeze had risen again to scatter the dry odor of sage up toward the house. Another cool gust caused both Adah and Jill to shudder. A single tumbleweed crawled across the prairie with the breeze until a clump of sagebrush slowed and halted its progress. The same gust that caused Jill and Adah to shudder blew the tumbleweed up and over the sage for about thirty feet before the wind died, and the tumbleweed floated to the ground to continue its deliberate progress across the prairie. The subtle breeze resumed, and Adah continued.

"Listen. In those old days, way back before the government came to Hanford and before Richland was even much of a town to speak of, there weren't too many folks living out this way. We had a place over yonder on the other side of the Yakima River."

She raised her arm and pointed in the direction of about a dozen recently constructed houses on dusty one-acre lots on the far side of the river. The lights in a few of the houses blinked on as the dusk deepened. Above the homes Jill could see where the prairie grass and sage had been replaced with deep green circles of alfalfa that rolled up to the very moment when the Horse Heaven

Hills bent sharply upward to meet the starry sky. From long circle irrigators that drew water from deep beneath the rocky soil, angel hair puffs of mineral-rich moisture nourished the hay, the last of the season's four cuttings.

"My daddy built us a house on the slope right there above the river. He never had any money, but he seemed to be able to get the material he needed to do the work. I was the youngest, but I had five brothers who helped as much as they could. I was pretty small in them days too, but there was always something I could do to help. We all did as much as we could."

Below the houses and the alfalfa fields, the riverbank was too steep for building or irrigation. The land there was brown and dry, as it must have been in the days of Adah's girlhood. In the near distance, the prairie seemed to fall away from the houses and into the river as the Yakima sped up and forked around a long, narrow, tree-covered island.

"Our place ain't there no more, but you can see where it was if you know where to look. Right there opposite the island, just where the steep part of the bank starts to level out some."

Jill could not see the river from where she sat with Adah, but she knew John's land turned downward to the river shore on the near bank. She could see where the land dropped away, and where it began to rise from the far bank. Adah's house had been only a short distance downstream from where she and Grady had entered the river.

"Weren't you sad about losing your place?"

"We never lost it. We left it. I married a young fella when I was fifteen. That's the way things happened in those times. There weren't much else to do but get married and get on with it. It weren't much like things is today."

"Did you love the boy…the boy you married?"

"Well, he weren't no boy, the way you might think. He was twenty-five. I might a' loved him. I reckon I must of. But I don't remember thinkin' too much about it. We didn't have time to think much about making up our minds. Seems like all folks these days do is worry themselves sick about makin' up their mind. The best way to go might be to take the road that's right there in front of you. Just go."

Jill thought about that. Everyone she knew was worried about what was going to happen years from now, as if the consequences of every choice would irreparably alter a future they could not hope to predict.

"Still, don't you miss it? Your old home? Your family? The old days? I remember the way things were before my dad died, but I can't remember everything, not everything I want to remember."

Adah studied the girl. Jill was no longer looking down. She was staring out across the valley, as if every memory she needed was out there above the sage and sand, between or beyond where she sat next to Adah and the Horse Heaven Hills, and if she looked hard enough, her past might come back to her.

"Some things I miss, I reckon. Me and my husband had a little house just up the hill, just there, above my folk's house. My brothers all lived nearby somewhere along the far bank of the river. Why, I had two babies by the time I was your age. One died right off. The other died later on. Then the man I married left. And I…"

"I don't think I could stand that. How could you stand losing your own children, your husband?"

"Like your momma? Well, you just do, that's all. There weren't nothin' to be done about it, so you stand it. And it wasn't all bad times. Seems like the bad times is all some folks want to remember. Like you and Grady. You all think you've lost so much, that you can't think about all the time you got left."

Jill felt the tug again. The Yakima was near enough. She calculated how long it would take her to walk to the river in the dark. Then she realized the water would not be deep enough, and the current would be too swift.

"Adah, sometimes I just don't want to go on. Sometimes it doesn't seem like there's any point at all. What did you have left after your children died and after your husband left?"

"I was a girl then, like you, so I had years and years. The years is just about all gone now, but I still got something to say, still got some stories to tell."

✳✳✳

Back in the house, John was in a somber mood. Jill pushed Adah in her chair back up the ramp into the house through the mudroom. John and Grady were sitting at the kitchen table, and

John was talking quietly. Jill was aware of tension in the room. She looked at Grady and made a questioning gesture with her hands. He shook his head. She rolled Adah to the table next to John and sat down next to Grady. Anne had gone back to her room when the dinner dishes were finished, but when she heard Jill and Adah come into the house, she came back into the kitchen and sat down at the far end of the table.

"You're going to do what you're going to do," John said. "I don't 'spect I can tell you not to go to Pendleton, but I ain't hopeful about what might happen down there."

"I know," Grady said. "I know what could happen every time I get on a bull. I ain't worried."

"What could happen?" Jill said.

"He could get hurt," John said.

"Or he could get killed," Adah said.

"Hurt? Killed?!" Jill said. "That doesn't scare you, Grady?"

Grady folded his hands and said nothing.

"He said he ain't worried," John said.

"Worried ain't the same as being scared," Adah said.

"Well, I'm goin' to Pendleton," he said. "Worried or scared, it don't matter. I'm goin'."

"I thought," Jill said in a quiet voice. "I thought we were going to leave together."

"What?!" Anne said. "You thought *what*?"

"What is she talkin' about, boy?" John asked.

Adah, put her hand on John's forearm and pressed down.

"Nothin'" Grady said. "We was just thinkin'."

"Were we just *thinkin'* down there by the river?" Jill said.

"Is this true?" Anne said. "You're seventeen! You can't just go off with a boy!" Anne paused and stared at her daughter. "You're confused. You don't know this boy."

"Jill, I'm sorry. I haven't … You don't know what could happen …"

Anne felt her lower jaw begin to shake, so she clinched her teeth and squeezed her eyes shut to suppress a sob. She was nearly overcome by an urge, biological in strength, to take Jill in her arms and squeeze love into her. But she held back because she could not remember the last time she had touched or even spoken her daughter affectionately. *What have I done?*

"Jill, baby, this is not what I've wanted … what your father wanted …" Anne cleared her throat to speak, but Adah interrupted.

"Well," the old woman said. "She's goin' to do what she's goin' to do. Right, John?"

Then she turned toward Anne and said, "I'm guessin' this here girl ain't done much a' nothin' for a good long time now, except maybe hide from you and everyone else. If she wants to go off with Grady here, I don't think there's any harm in that."

"But what will people think?" Anne said. "I can make this right. Jill, I can make this right. We'll go home. Jill needs to go back to school."

"Mom, we're in the middle of freakin' nowhere. No one cares."

Anne pointed an accusing finger at Grady. "You don't *know* this boy."

Grady shrugged.

"I knew him in school, Mom. It's okay."

"No, it's not okay." She walked over to her daughter and put her hands on her shoulders. "I've not been any kind of mother since your father died." She shot Grady the kind of disgusted look that revealed what people in larger towns often think of country people, and then turned to Jill. "I'm your mother and I'm telling you that you are *not* going away with this boy." She dropped her hands and looked at John. "Can you take us back to Richland in the morning? We've imposed on you long enough. Jill, come with me so we can pack to leave."

John didn't move a muscle.

"Mom, I'm leaving with Grady. It's not what you think."

Anne didn't respond. Instead, she left the kitchen quickly and went down the hall to the room she shared with her daughter. Seconds later they heard a closet door open, and Anne pulling suitcases from the closet.

Adah turned to Jill. "Do what your momma says, girl."

Jill's jaw dropped. "But you just said there's no harm in us leaving—"

"Your momma's still your momma, and you got to do what she says. Go on an' pack." Jill wasn't certain, but she thought Adah might have winked at her as she left the room.

The old woman followed Jill down the hall, leaving the men in the kitchen. John walked out the back door, while Grady stood at the counter, alone and confused.

CHAPTER 11

Grady sat in John's truck and waited for Jill for more than an hour. Sometime after midnight, the passenger-side door opened, and Jill started to push a pink suitcase and a military-style duffle bag onto the front seat.

"Throw them in the backseat," he said. "Not much room up here.

She did as she was told and climbed up into the passenger seat. He started the truck and drove carefully along the dirt and gravel road that led from the house to the gate he'd opened for John the night he arrived. He stopped the truck at the gate.

"There's a chain on that gate. It's always locked."

"Maybe not. I'll look."

"No, you stay here. It's locked."

Grady got out of the truck. He reached behind the driver's seat and pulled out a heavy set of bolt cutters.

"I grabbed these from the barn before we left," he said.

The gate and the paved road on the other side were illuminated by the headlights. He used the bolt cutters to sever a single link in the chain and pulled it away from the gate.

He held up the lock and severed chain so Jill could see. He let the gate fall open, got back in, with the lock and chain still in his hand, and drove through the gate. He stopped, closed the gate, replaced the chain, and tied the severed links together with a length of bailing twine so it would remain closed.

As he hopped back in the cab, she asked, "Will John come after us? He sided with my mom, didn't he? Adah thought what we're doing is okay."

"Maybe. But he don't know where we're goin'. I don't know about Adah. She don't see things the same as most people."

Grady drove through Benton City and stopped for fuel at the Conoco station. He filled the tank and pulled onto the interstate. He drove another fifteen miles before he pulled off the highway in Richland.

"Where are we going?" she asked.

"My mom's place. Got to get some things." He parked the truck in front of his mother's house. "Come on. I'll need your help."

She followed him into the house and down the short hallway to a cluttered extra bedroom used for storage. Among the usual boxes, she noticed two saddles and at least two dozen ornate belt buckles arranged on a shelf.

"What are those?" she said, pointing to the shelf.

"Buckles. Most are my dad's. Couple are mine. It's what you get when you win a rodeo. Buckles are nice, but the check that comes with 'em is better."

"So, what do you need from here?"

"Campin' stuff. Tent. Stove. Sleepin' bags. Stuff like that. We'll get food in Pomeroy in the morning."

"Pomeroy?"

"Here put these in the truck."

Grady handed Jill two nylon sleeping bags, and she started down the hallway. He followed with a tent in a large nylon case. When they returned to the storage room, he handed her a small, green camp stove. He gathered up several propane bottles and put them in a box with an aluminum cook kit and a large box of matches. They put the second load in the truck and both climbed in. He started the engine.

"Wait here," he said. "I need one more thing." Grady went back into the house. He returned to the truck with an old-fashioned lever action rifle and a box of ammunition.

"What do you need that for?"

He stored the rifle and ammunition in the backseat.

"Don't know," he said. "My dad always said it was better to have a tool and not need it, than to need somethin' and not have it. We may need this rifle."

"Where are we going?"

"The Blue Mountains."

He pulled away from the curb and returned to the freeway. In five minutes, they were out of Richland and crossing the Columbia heading toward Pasco. After another ten miles, they crossed the Snake River at its confluence with the Columbia. After fifteen more miles, they turned away from the river onto Highway 12 and headed toward Walla Walla and the Blue Mountains.

"Can you turn the heater on?" The night was warm, but Jill suddenly felt cold. She looked out the passenger-side window and whispered, "What am I doing?"

She had never slept outdoors or even been on a date, but she was leaving in the middle of the night with a boy she had just met, a boy who rode bulls for a living, owned a gun, and apparently knew how to use it. A week earlier she hadn't been aware that such people existed. Questions flooded her mind as the truck rumbled on down the dark corridor of Highway 12 away from the same Columbia River that had nearly taken her life. Was she scared? Yes. Was she excited? A little. Was she curious? Absolutely.

Highway 12 was a mostly two-lane road that began in Aberdeen, Washington at the point of Gray's Harbor. It wandered somewhat aimlessly at times through the Cascade Mountains before it swept down off White Pass and into the Yakima River Valley. Seventy-five miles later it crossed the Snake River at Pasco and turned a little south along the Columbia River before it angled sharply east toward Walla Walla. The narrow highway seemed to deliberately skirt the state's major population centers, as if it preferred the solitude of the rugged mountains and the loneliness of the sage prairies.

Jill had settled in against the passenger-side door and turned sideways so she could watch Grady drive. By 1:30 in the morning and about eight miles west of Walla Walla, they passed a sign saying the Whitman Mission Historical Site was ahead on the right. Jill remembered a bit from school about the mission. She knew that Marcus and Narcissa Whitman lived there before they were killed. She couldn't remember why. *But there must have been a reason*, she thought. *Isn't there always a reason?* She thought about Narcissa, the young woman who traveled all the way from Massachusetts to live in the wilderness with Marcus. Jill could not imagine traveling all that way for a man, or for anything else.

"I wonder if she loved him," she said. But Grady was staring at the dark roadway.

"Huh?"

She spoke louder, "I wonder if that Whitman woman loved her husband, or if there was some other reason for coming all the way out here. What do people do in a mission anyway?"

"I don't guess it matters much," he said. "I don't guess she thought about it. She probably just did it. People didn't think about things so much back then. I reckon she just made up her mind and did it. Kinda like what we're doin."

He sounded like Adah.

"But it was a mistake," she said. "She died right back there. I think she lost a baby too. The baby girl drowned in the river."

"I don't know. Maybe she thought about it and maybe she didn't, but the thing is she did it. That's what my dad said all the time. Got to get things done. Can't think about what to do too much."

"No!" she shouted. The harsh reply startled Grady.

"No," she said again, her voice falling to a near whisper. "There has to be a reason."

She turned back to the window and watched the dark countryside pass by and said, "I wish I knew."

Just as they were about to enter Walla Walla, she saw the lights of the state prison about a quarter of mile off the highway to the north.

"What's that?" she said.

"I guess that must be the prison. Let's take a look."

The Washington State Penitentiary at Walla Walla had a well-deserved reputation for being one of the toughest prisons in the country. A serial killer from Los Angeles, they called him "The Hillside Strangler," was caught after he killed two college students in Bellingham, Washington. The story goes that he was given a choice between being tried in Washington and serving his time in Walla Walla or confessing to the California murders and spending the rest of his life in a California prison. The killer confessed in order to stay out of Walla Walla. The prison was also the site of Washington's rarely used death row. People on the highway often felt ill at ease when they drove by the brightly lit prison grounds at night.

Grady pulled the truck off the road into the narrow, gravel parking lot of a closed roadside vegetable stand adorned with fading, hand-painted signs advertising "Walla Walla Sweet Onions and Asparagus," and parked parallel to the highway. He got out and leaned against the warm hood of the truck. He stared at the prison and wondered what his father was doing. Jill got out and walked to the rear of the truck. She leaned her folded arms on the flatbed and watched Grady while the boy stared at the prison.

"What is it?" she asked.

"Nothing really," he said. "It's just…just that…My dad's in there, and I wonder what he's doin' right now."

"He's probably sleeping or locked up in a cell," she said. "I don't guess they probably get to stay up late and watch TV or anything like that."

"That's not what I meant exactly," he said. "But I wonder what it's been like for him to live there for the last six years."

He stared at the hard-packed gravel surface of the parking lot and dug at the stubborn tuft of a grassy weed with the toe of his boot. A car sped by on the highway, trailing a cool breeze that made Jill shudder. He raised his head, gazing at the prison's bright lights, which obscured the stars. A semi-rig lumbered by, and the ground shook. A rear tire escaped the pavement, and a brief explosion of dust and pebbles caused Jill to turn away and cover her face. When the truck was gone and the dust had settled, Grady got a dim glimpse of the stars directly overhead.

He felt a dull ache coming from the same deep spot where the rage had been, the same rage he'd used on the kid in Richland. He sank to his haunches.

Jill walked around the rear of the truck and approached him carefully. She stopped and waited at the passenger-side door, took one more step, and lowered herself to her knees next to him, exactly one arm's length away.

She reached out and touched him. He flinched slightly then allowed her to rub his shoulder. With her outstretched hand, she leaned farther forward and gently stroked his cheek with the back of her fingers.

She straightened up and glanced across the road at the brightly lit prison walls and shimmering razor wire. She walked around the front of the truck and got back in. Grady got up, opened the driver-side door, and climbed into the cab. He slid forward, put his head back and closed his eyes.

"I'm tired," he said. "Maybe we should sit here for a while and get a little rest."

She said nothing. Instead, she moved toward him and laid her head in his lap. He put his hand on her shoulder, and they slept until the sun came up.

***

It was full daylight when Grady woke Jill. They drove into Walla Walla and had breakfast at an all-night restaurant just off the second exit.

"How much farther?" she asked.

"Sixty, maybe sixty-five miles to Pomeroy. Then we head south into the Blues, maybe twenty miles. We should find a place to set up camp sometime before noon."

"I've never been camping."

"It's easy once you get set up. Won't be anyone around 'less we run into a hunter or something."

From Walla Walla to Clarkston, Highway 12 divided the Palouse Hills in a long northeasterly arc that formed the northern boundary of the Blue Mountain region in Washington's far southeastern corner. Travelers who left Highway 12 to explore the pristine wilderness south and east of the tiny towns along the road could have wandered on foot for days before they encountered credible evidence of civilization. There was talk of widening and improving the roads that ran off to the south into the Blues. Two lanes could be treacherous in the mountains, especially during the winter and particularly at night. But the people in Washington's three most southeasterly counties were jealous of their wilderness traditions and close-to-the-land way of life and resisted the temptation to develop the land in the mountains south of Highway 12.

One such southbound byway, Peola Road, climbed gently away from the tiny town of Pomeroy. After seventeen miles the road became an anomaly on the map, the only state highway in

Washington that was not paved. Twenty-five miles from town, even the gravel road ended deep in the Umatilla National Forest, replaced by a primitive network of dirt tracks barely wide enough for a single vehicle. Still, someone who knew the roads and understood the risks inherent to driving in the mountains without a map could have made his way from Highway 12 to small towns in northeastern Oregon like Joseph and Enterprise and from there could've linked up with more civilized roadways.

After seventy-five minutes they reached Pomeroy, the seat of the least populated county in Washington. At the east end of town, Grady turned onto Peola Road and headed south through miles of rolling hills covered with wheat into the Blue Mountains. The paved road eventually turned to gravel, and the wheat fields bled into the forest at the forked junction of two dirt tracks.

"My dad used to get work down here every fall," he said. "We'd all come, my mom and my dad and me. I used to go with my dad when he went huntin' in these mountains. I'm pretty sure we take the west fork. Seems like I remember him goin' to the right here, then the road turns back to the east. I guess we'll see."

They had passed the last farmhouse five miles back.

"You're not sure?" Jill said. "Does anyone live down here."

"Not that I've ever heard of. This country ain't changed since forever. We need to find a place to camp for a coupla days."

He got out of the truck and locked the hubs so he could engage the four-wheel drive. He took the fork on the right and headed slowly into the wilderness of the Umatilla National Forest.

As the road narrowed and the forest closed in, Jill moved away from the door to the middle of the seat and turned so she could see the forest passing by outside the open passenger-side window. Tree limbs brushed the side of the truck, and fragrant bits of pine needles and fir fronds fell through the side window and onto the seat. She slid farther away from the door toward Grady.

"Do you think we should go back?" she said.

He did not answer. She turned to face the windshield. Her hands were trembling. After another mile he stopped the truck. To their left the roadway disappeared and the narrow vista of an unnamed canyon opened below them. Grady did not move, but Jill got out and walked to the front of the truck.

The morning sunbathed the canyon in a filtered light that revealed more than a dozen foliate shades of green. As she gazed at the valley, she noticed the vegetation in the near distance remained verdant even as it darkened to near black in the haze at the far end. Her mind was blank until the title of an old song her mother used to listen to popped into her mind. *Evergreen.* Jill thought. *Ever. Green.* She put one hand on the warm hood of the truck. She had stopped trembling.

Then again, she remembered something about the Blue Mountains from school or from a book she'd read. Something about Indians and gold and a war. There was a movie with a dignified actor making a speech at the end. Something about not fighting. Something about forever. She remembered the river, and she remembered her father.

"Forever," she whispered.

She got back in the truck. She faced the front, but turned toward Grady and said, "This road scares me."

"I know," he said. "It's the only way, though."

She rolled up the window and settled back into the seat. "Drive."

***

As Grady drove, the road continued to climb for another mile, then turned sharply left and dipped down toward the canyon. When the road leveled out, he pulled the truck into a flat clearing with a fire pit already laid out. Behind the clearing fifty yards and down a hill was a substantial stream that gurgled off the hillside and through a culvert beneath the gravel road.

He climbed out of the truck and began to unload the tent and other camping gear, several grocery bags, and a big box of food they'd bought in Pomeroy. He took the rifle from the backseat and leaned it against the large nylon bag that held the tent.

Jill walked into the middle of the clearing and stopped. At the back of the clearing the forest resumed and the landscape climbed gently for about two-hundred feet then became steeper. She could see farther in each direction than she thought would be possible because the trees were spaced far apart, and the undergrowth was sparse. Back at home, houses were close together. Familiar streets and people she knew defined her surroundings. What she remembered most about school was the mild claustrophobia she felt as hundreds of kids crowded into the narrow hallways between classes. She stood in the center of this cleared spot in the mountains and realized the only sign of previous human activity was a shallow hole in the ground surrounded by charred rocks. She turned around full circle, taking in the grand emptiness of the Blue Mountains. As far as she knew, she and Grady were the only people for many miles in every direction.

"I thought it would be cold," she said. The morning had waned, and it would be a hot day.

"It will be," he said. "At night it might get down close to freezin'. But if it don't storm, the days should be nice enough."

"How long will we be here?"

"I got to be in Pendleton Wednesday. We can stay here the whole time or we can go south or east. It's two or three hours east to Anatone. Then the paved road goes down into Oregon, to Joseph or Enterprise. And only an hour back to Pomeroy. We got most of a full tank of diesel and plenty of food."

She walked to the edge of the clearing and traversed the entire extent of the outer edges of her new world. She had never been in such a place, and it seemed important that she recognize the boundary between the clearing and the wilderness. The road came up hard against the east side of the clearing. She stood near the road and looked out at the same canyon she had seen earlier from higher up. They were still above the canyon floor, but now she could make out much more than just vague shades of green. The brown canyon floor was now visible. The stream emerged from the culvert on the far side of the road and dropped in a shallow cascade into the steep stream bed below.

She turned back and saw that Grady was done unloading the truck. He had pulled the tent out of the bag, and it was lying flat, about thirty feet from the fire pit. He had assembled two long fiberglass poles and was running them through nylon loops at the top of the tent in an X pattern.

"It'll be easier if you help me with the tent," he said.

"I don't know what to do."

"Just hold one end of these supports while I stick the other end into the corner of the tent."

She did as she was told. When he had one corner secured, he took the other end of the pole from her and stuck it into the corner at the opposite side. They repeated the process at the other two corners, and the tent was up.

"That was really easy," she said, pleased with herself.

"Not quite done," he said. He pounded four metal tent stakes into the ground a few feet from each corner. Then he tied each stake to the tent with a thin nylon cord, which he pulled tight and secured with a metal bracket. He walked slowly around the tent, double checking to make sure each stake was secure.

"Is there anything I can do?" she asked.

"Yeah. Take all the food that's not in cans out of the paper bags and put it in the big metal cooler, except the bread. Try not to break the bag of ice that's in there. It'll last longer in the bag. I'm goin' to get firewood."

She started to transfer the food, but when she looked up from her work, he was gone, and so was the rifle.

"Grady," she said. "Where are you?" Her voice was soft, almost a whisper, because she was afraid to shout. She felt the skin on the back of her neck begin to tighten as she put the last of the food in the cooler. When she was done, she climbed into the truck and locked the doors. She looked out at the clearing and at the empty spaces between the evergreen trees. *Where am I supposed to pee?*

Grady returned after about twenty minutes with a large load of sticks and small logs in one arm. He was carrying the rifle with his other hand. He dropped his load near the fire pit and leaned the rifle against the cooler. Jill got out of the truck.

"What were you doing in the truck?"

"Nothing." She tried but couldn't keep the barest hint of a whine out of her voice. "Just sitting."

"Sittin'?"

"I don't want to be left by myself. I can help you carry stuff."

"Okay. But now we have enough firewood to at least get some food heated up later."

She nodded toward the gun. "Why'd you take that with you? What would you need it for?"

"Probably nothing. But we're not in town. There's no one to call if there's trouble."

She frowned.

"I don't mean *trouble,* but if there's a problem."

"If there are animals out there, something dangerous, then I really don't want to be left alone."

He watched her. "I didn't think you'd be scared."

"I'm not scared. I've never done anything like this. I don't know what might happen."

"Okay," he said. "I get it. I don't know what might happen either."

∗∗∗

Early that morning, Adah was in the kitchen, and John had gone outside to do the morning chores when Anne came down the hall in a rush.

"Jill?" she said. "Adah, do you know where Jill is?"

"I haven't seen her this morning. Didn't figure she'd be up yet."

John came in through the mudroom and saw that Anne was in the kitchen.

"I guess I won't be taking you into town," he said. "Looks like that boy took my truck. Frank'll be out later today. I reckon he can take you and Jill home."

Adah sat in her chair, smirking.

"What is it?" he said.

"Adah, what do you know?" Anne said with panic rising in her voice.

"I don't know nothin' you don't know," she said.

John leaned back against the kitchen counter and pushed his hat back on his head.

"Jill went with him," Anne said. "Didn't she? Well, we've got to go after them. Or call the police."

"I don't know where they're likely to go," John said. "The sheriff could probably find my truck unless they headed up to the mountains or somewhere."

"Mountains?" Anne said. "Do you think they're not coming back here?"

"I don't spect so," Adah said. "I think those younguns was just starting to get acquainted. You heard what Jill said last night."

"She said they were going to…Oh my Lord! We've got to find them!" Anne was trying to get her voice back under control.

"I'll call the sheriff," he said. "They can look for my truck."

"No, John," Adah said. "Wait."

Everyone was silent.

"Anne, honey, what did you bring that girl out here for?"

Anne wiped her eyes with her fingertips.

"We were…We hadn't…For a long time…We'd been … Jill had … For years. Ever since…"

"Ever since your husband died and Jill lost her father."

"Yes. Ever since then, we've been … numb."

"And?" Adah prompted.

"And I thought with a change, a new place, different people, we might be able to get our lives going again. Then Jill runs off with this boy, a rodeo cowboy."

"Well then," Adah said. "I guess she ain't numb no more."

***

"We ain't ate since early this morning," Grady said.

"What time is it?"

"Don't know. Don't guess it matters."

He took two canvas folding chairs out of the backseat of the truck and set them on the ground on opposite sides of the fire pit. Jill sat in one of the chairs and watched him. There was a heavy steel cooking grate, blackened by years of use, on the ground. Grady leaned the grate against the rocks that encircled the fire pit.

"We won't build a fire until it gets close to dark," he said. "Firewood's not easy to come by."

"Seems like there'd be lots of wood around."

"This spot looks like it's been used a lot. Most of the wood nearby has been gathered up and burned already. There's plenty a' wood, but none of its very close."

"Well, I'm not hungry anyway."

"I am."

He pulled a loaf of white bread out of a paper grocery bag. He opened the cooler and pulled out a package of sliced ham and a small squeeze bottle of mustard. He squeezed a generous amount of mustard onto two slices of the bread. He ripped open the ham and removed several slices and slapped them onto one of the slices of bread. He plopped the other slice of bread onto the ham. He devoured the entire sandwich in three or four bites.

"We could go for a little hike," he said while he made a second sandwich. She noticed that the package of sliced ham was nearly gone. "Maybe walk up the road a little. You ain't really got shoes that'll be useful on a mountain trail."

He ate his second sandwich more slowly. She looked down at her thin canvas shoes and remembered she was wearing the only shoes she'd brought from Richland. She wished she had more substantial footwear.

"OK," she said. "Maybe."

He finished off his sandwich and wiped his hands on his jeans. He tossed the remains of the ham back into the cooler. He carried it to the truck and set it on the backseat.

"Bring the bag with the bread," he said. She brought the bag to him, and he set it on the floor next to a cardboard box filled with canned soup and chili and instant mac-and-cheese. He closed and locked the door.

"Let's go."

He started off up the road. She followed but had to run a few steps to catch up. Once she was next to him, he slowed down, and they strolled away from the clearing. The road dropped gently, and after a few minutes, she could no longer hear the stream.

After about half a mile, they had nearly reached the canyon floor.

"Can we stop for a while?" she said. "It seems like we've been moving all day and all last night."

The floor of the broad canyon rose up steeply to meet the road. At the bottom was a lush meadow, with only one or two widely spaced trees. Jill thought she could see a small lake or pond in the distance, but she wasn't certain. They sat about two feet apart on a log that served as a barrier between the road and the canyon and looked down across the meadow at the bottom toward a rugged bulge that seemed swell up out of the south end of the canyon.

"Does that hill have a name?" she asked.

"I think that must be Mount Misery."

"Misery. Why misery?"

"I think it must have somethin' to do with the weather down here. I hear it can get right nasty in winter. Someone probably spent a winter in misery on that mountain and named it when spring came. In a day or two we'll drive over into Asotin County past Mt. Horrible on the way to Anatone."

They sat silently for a long time, and then Grady put his hand on Jill's shoulder and began to massage her thin neck. She turned toward him but did not move closer. She let him rub her neck for a short time then she leaned away so he'd know to remove his hand. She crossed her legs and folded her hands in her lap. She squinted against the glare reflecting off the emerald expanse of the meadow and the mountain in the distance. He reached out and put his hand on her chin and turned her face toward him. Silent tears ran down her cheeks.

"Jill, I…" he said." I didn't mean anything. I only…"

She put her hand on his wrist but did not push his hand away.

"I'm glad we're here together, Grady. I really am. I just want to be with you. I think I need to be with you, but that's all."

"That'll do for me," he said. "I didn't mean nothin'."

"Well, it's not exactly *nothin'*. We're out here, aren't we? Alone. In the woods. Grady, I've never even been on a date. You're my first *date*."

He laughed and stood up.

"I'll be good. I promise," he said. Grady turned away and stared at the mountain in the purple distance. He could hear the breeze rustle the tress on the hillside across the road. He closed his eyes and breathed in the gentle pungency of the pines mingled with the familiar odor of road dust. He turned back toward Jill. "I'd promise your dad if I could."

He extended his hand, and she took it, and he pulled her to her feet.

They returned to the clearing. Grady busied himself cutting up firewood with a small axe and a handsaw while she looked around nervously.

"Um," she said. "I think I'm going to go take a look at the stream for a minute. You stay here, okay?"

"Huh?" he said. "Stay close. Make sure you can see the camp."

"And you make sure you don't see."

"Oh." He grinned. "You got to pee. I'll stay over here by the truck."

She walked gingerly 50 yards downhill to the stream, careful not to let her feet slide away on the steep spots. The afternoon had grown very hot, and she hadn't had a chance to get clean since late the day before. When she reached the water, she was pleased to discover a shallow pool. She double checked to make sure she was hidden from Grady's view then found a spot about thirty yards downstream from the pool and relieved herself.

She returned to the pool and removed her shoes and socks and waded into the water. The bottom of the pool was sandy, so she waded to the middle where the water reached her thighs and soaked her jeans. The water in the pool was clear enough that she could see the bottom except where her careful footsteps roiled the sand and clouded the water around her legs. If she stood very still, though, the slight current would take the cloudiness away. She ran her fingertips across the surface, then bent down and splashed water on her face. She made her way back to the bank and stepped out.

She made sure Grady was otherwise occupied. As promised, he was at the far side organizing something in the backseat of the truck. She returned to the bank and carefully removed her jeans and tee shirt so that she was standing in nothing but her underwear. She took one more look back up the hill toward the clearing and dropped her bra and stepped out of her panties.

She returned to the center of the pool and lowered her body until the water reached her chin. She leaned back with her head pointed upstream and spread her arms. She closed her eyes and held her nose and exhaled through her mouth. She felt herself sink onto the sandy bottom, opened her eyes, and recognized the glare of the sun shining through the trees and onto the surface of the pool.

She sat up and shook the water away from her face and let the slow current wash around her. She stood up and water dripped down from her hair and over her naked body. She thought about the two other times she had been submerged recently, alone in the Columbia River on a rainy night and in the Yakima River with Grady on a warm afternoon. She didn't know what the connection was, but there seemed to be one. Adah had used a word to describe her life. What was it?

"Grace," she said aloud. "Grace." *It's got nothing to do with what you've done or what's been done to you. It only has to do with who you are.*

She looked downstream. She could see Mount Misery in the distance between the trees.

"Mount Misery. Terrible name," she said. "Doesn't seem quite right … from here."

She returned to the bank and dried off as best she could with her tee shirt. She put her wet clothes back on and returned to the clearing. Grady was busy arranging small sticks in the bottom of the fire pit on top of a ripped-up paper bag. When she came back up the hill into the clearing, he stood up. He could see she was wet.

"You fall in?"

She walked up to him, put her arms around his neck, raised herself up on her toes, and kissed him on the lips. She lowered herself and put her head against his chest. He responded by putting his arms around her, and they stood that way for a long time.

"Grace," she whispered.

"What you say?"

She stepped away from him and headed for the truck.

"Nothing. Let's eat."

✳✳✳

Adah, John, and Anne were speaking with a tall deputy sheriff outside the house. He handed John the severed chain from the gate.

"Looks like he cut the chain with a bolt cutter," the deputy said. "Tied the chain back up with a bailing twine. Any of you folks have any idea where these two kids might a' gone?"

"I heard Grady say somethin' about White Pass," Adah said from her chair.

"White Pass?" Anne said. "Isn't that over by Yakima?"

"About seventy miles west of Yakima," the deputy said. "If they headed up that way, they'll have to stay on the main highway until they find a place to camp. Even then, most of the campsites are right off the highway. They won't be hard to find if they went that way."

"She's only seventeen," Anne said in shaky voice. "She's never been away."

"Happens more often than you'd think," the deputy said. "We'll let the Yakima sheriff know and the state patrol. John's truck isn't going to be easy to hide. Kids don't usually think these things through."

"I just want her back," Anne said. "Can we get that boy jailed?"

"Well, it doesn't sound to me like he forced her. If she went willingly…"

"Just make them come back. Please."

The deputy held open his car door. "We'll watch for 'em, ma'am. But I bet they'll be back on their own before we have a chance to look around much."

He got into his car and left. John turned away and headed toward the barn.

"That boy didn't say nothin' about White Pass or Yakima," he said as he walked away.

"What?" Anne said. "John, what did you say?"

He stopped and turned around. "Boy's going to be in Pendleton next Wednesday. I wonder why he'd tell Adah he's going west, when Pendleton's a hundred miles the other way. I don't think Grady would lie." He continued into the barn.

"Don't pay him no mind. That old man can't even read a map. They went wherever they went, and they'll be back whenever they get back," Adah said. "Give me a hand here, dearie. I could walk, but I'm feeling a little weak today. Push me back around the house and up the ramp. You look like you could use a cup a' hot coffee."

Anne watched John walk away then pushed Adah's chair to the back of the house and up the ramp through the mudroom into the kitchen.

"You get us some coffee," Adah said. "Meet me at the table."

Anne took two mugs from the cabinet and poured coffee into one for Adah and filled one for herself.

"I wouldn't be too worried about your girl. Grady's been on his own a lot. His daddy ain't been around for a while, so I 'spect he's had to grow up faster'n most. He's no fool anyway."

Anne put her mug down. "She's seventeen. She's too young."

"Among the folks you know, that's probably true. But she also ain't so young neither."

"Adah, she's had no time to grow up! She's had …She's had to deal with…"

"With her daddy dyin'. I know. But honey, I'm going to say some things that'll be hard for you to hear. Her daddy dyin' ain't the worst thing that's happened to that girl."

Anne leaned back and slumped into her chair. She thought she would cry, but after a quiet moment, she sat up straight and held her right fist against her mouth.

"Don't say nothin' for a minute," Adah said. "I told Jill a story. Told her about my growin' up down there across the river. By the time I was seventeen, I'd already lost two babies and the third was on the way. I had a no-count husband who's about to light out, Huck Finn like. And I weren't no smarter and no more grown up than your girl."

"I haven't been there for her, Adah. I never…I never gave her chance to…"

"To remember her daddy and to grieve proper."

Adah stood up and leaned across the table and took Anne's left hand in her right. The two women watched each other for a long moment.

"I know," Anne said. "I haven't done anything to help her. But now, I just don't want anything to happen to her. I don't know how much more she can handle."

Adah tugged gently on her arm.

"You ain't listened," she whispered. Then, louder, she said, "That girl can handle whatever she has to handle. We're all built that way. Sometimes we just need someone else to—"

"Show the way?"

"Or let it be. Let it be and watch 'em go off on their own. Folks who get where they're 'sposed to, sometimes get there by goin' the way we don't want 'em to."

Anne sat back down. Adah remained standing, leaning on both hands.

"I know. Maybe you're right."

Adah smiled and shook her head.

"Things *is* goin' to happen, dear. But for a reason and for a purpose and for the best."

CHAPTER 12

Jill climbed into the front seat off the truck and pulled dry clothes out of her bag. She made sure Grady was on the other side of the clearing before she removed her wet clothes and put on dry jeans and a tee shirt. He had said the temperature would be likely to drop later, so she pulled her oversized sweatshirt out of the bag.

He had a fire going among the small sticks in the fire pit. He had piled logs of various sizes closer to the fire. As it grew and burned down, he added larger logs. On the cooler, which he had moved near the fire, sat two large potatoes wrapped in tin foil.

"Why'd you start the fire so soon?" Jill asked. "It's not cold yet."

"You can stay warm without a fire," he said. "But it ain't no fun to eat a cold dinner when you're campin'. In a while, they'll be a nice bed of coals, and we'll bury those potatoes in the fire and let 'em bake. I got some hamburger and some nice big sausages to go with the potatoes. Be about an hour or so."

She realized she had not eaten since breakfast in Walla Walla shortly after sunrise. She was very hungry. "Is there something I can eat in the meantime?"

"There's bread and mustard in the bag in the truck and sliced turkey in the cooler. Make a sandwich."

She gathered everything she needed from the truck and the cooler and made a sandwich. Her cheeks puffed out as she wolfed it down and looked around for something to drink. She found a half gallon of milk and two large bottles of orange juice in the cooler. She knew there were paper cups in the truck, but she took a long drink of the orange juice straight from a bottle.

"What's left to do?" she asked.

"Get the sleeping bags and put them in the tent."

Jill retrieved the two sleeping bags from the truck. She untied and unrolled them inside the tent and spread them out along opposite walls, about six feet apart.

"There's more room in there than it looks like from the outside," she said when she came out of the tent. "The ground's hard too."

Grady was putting more wood on the fire. "You'll get used to it."

Later they ate a messy dinner. Thick hamburger patties sizzled in a cast-iron skillet, and the baked potatoes from the fire stayed hot in the foil. When they were finished, Grady burned their paper plates in the fire, folded the tin foil and stored it in the box, and poured water from the stream into the skillet, which was still on the grate.

"It'll boil itself clean."

"I don't think so," Jill said. "That water looks pretty gross."

"It'll be clean enough."

She shrugged. "I guess."

The sun began to set while they sat quietly in the folding chairs, one on each side of the fire. Grady sat with his elbows on his knees. It appeared to Jill that he was closely examining the ground between his feet. She thought that was a little strange. But, she thought, *there's really nothing else to do*. Normally at this time of day, she would be sitting in her room trying to think of something to do that didn't involve anyone else. But here, in the quiet of the near wilderness, she discovered she didn't want anything else to do.

She inhaled the pleasant smell of the burning wood in the fire. "I saw you get into a fight once in school," she said. "There was this big jock-type kid. He said something about your boots or your hat or something. I don't know. But when he started to push you, you hit him three times in the face. I remember it was three times and he went down hard. Then two of his friends tried to grab you and then the principal came, and they took you to the office."

"Yeah," he said. "I remember. Hard not to. I probably should a' only hit him once. Or maybe not at all."

"The police came later, but I never heard what happened and I never saw you around school again."

"They took me into the office. Told me I was to sit there and wait. No one came around for a long time, so I left and walked home. Didn't seem like anything good was goin' to happen if I stayed. They called my mom later. They told her I couldn't come back to school until we all had a meeting. The police came that night. Told us that I'd probably be arrested when the kid's folks pressed charges. Guess they never did 'cause I never heard nothin', and I never went back to school."

"You've been in a lot fights, haven't you?"

"Maybe, I guess."

She picked up her chair without standing up all the way and turned it toward him. "Why do you get into fights? The way you've been since last night, the way you were at the meadow, it doesn't seem like you'd fight."

He was silent. The sun had set, but the autumn dusk lingered. Jill felt the cold begin to settle, but the heat of the fire made her sweatshirt unnecessary.

"But I do fight," he said.

"Maybe you shouldn't."

He turned to her. "Maybe you shouldn't cover yourself up like you do."

She shrugged. "Could be, I guess."

They stared into fire until it was completely dark, not saying another word.

Finally, Grady said Jill should go into the tent first and get into her sleeping bag. She took her shoes off, put on her sweatshirt, and crawled into the sleeping bag she'd laid out to the left the tent flap. She snuggled down and squirmed around until she found a semi-comfortable position on the hard ground. She could hear Grady milling around outside. She heard a door of the truck open and close. Then he came into the tent. Moonlight filtered by the trees shined through the thin nylon tent fabric. She watched while he removed his boots and set them against the back wall of the tent. He slid down into his sleeping bag, turned over once to face away from Jill and did not stir.

Jill's eyes were heavy, but she did not sleep. She was warmer than she thought she would be in the sleeping bag, so she removed her sweatshirt and rolled it up to use as a pillow. She lay on her back with her eyes open and listened. She could hear the stream, and a slight breeze rustled the trees. She heard Grady breathing.

Later she was startled by a momentary scraping noise like something being dragged over rock or metal. Then she heard what might have been two or three heavy footsteps. Finally, all she could hear was the stream and the wind in the trees.

She crawled carefully out of her sleeping bag and rearranged it next to Grady. When she climbed back in, it was still warm. The sound of his breathing was a little louder, and the sound of the stream and the wind in the trees seemed farther away. She turned on her side to face him, closed her eyes, and went to sleep.

The next morning after a breakfast of scrambled eggs and campfire toast, which reminded her of a meal in Adah's kitchen, they drove slowly east to the tiny town of Anatone, then south on the paved road to Joseph, Oregon. They filled the truck with diesel and walked up and down the quiet main street of the little town named for the Nez Pearce Indian chief who had fought a war with the US Cavalry for possession of the Blue Mountains.

They spent the next two nights in an Oregon State Park campground in the foothills, eating breakfast in the camp and returning to Joseph to eat indoors at dinnertime. She was comforted by their proximity to Joseph yet found herself wishing they were back in their isolated clearing.

On the fourth day, they drove to La Grande, Oregon, and from there took Interstate 84 to Pendleton. They spent the night before Grady's ride at the Round-Up at the Super 8 in a room with two beds.

***

Grady's mother, Beth, was not a plain woman, but she had not taken much care of her appearance since her husband left. This day was different. The first night Grady spent with John and Adah, Beth drove to Walla Walla and slept in a motel near the Washington State Penitentiary. When she checked in, the desk clerk seemed to know why she was there but didn't say anything. She woke up early and spent a lot of time getting dressed. She put on a new dress and carefully applied modest makeup for the first time in many years.

By noon she sat in a small room outside the assistant warden's office, waiting to see her husband, Grady Sr., after six years apart.

They had exchanged letters, and there had been secret (to Grady) phone calls, but her husband had insisted she not come to visit. He was in prison, he said, but he would not be there forever.

"Mrs. Cross," a tall secretary with a pleasant smile spoke to her. "The assistant warden will see you now."

Beth stood and followed the woman into the office. The assistant warden stood and extended his hand across the desk. He introduced himself, offered her a chair, and left the room. She sat in one of the two soft chairs and crossed her ankles.

He was gone for less than a minute. "Mrs. Cross. Is that still your name? Sorry, but these days, I have to ask."

"Yes. I'm still married to my husband."

"Mrs. Cross, as I told you when I telephoned, your husband is being paroled a week from Wednesday. He asked that we contact you, so you and he could meet with you before his release date.

"His sentence was ten years, but he's been a model inmate and, in his condition…"

"His condition?"

"Oh, my. He hasn't told you."

The warden paused. Beth could see he was gathering his thoughts, but she could not guess what thoughts he might be gathering. So, she waited.

"About a year ago now, there was an accident. A number of inmates were taken to the Blue Mountains to fight a fire. On the way home, the prison van rolled off the road in the dark. Your husband's legs were pinned beneath the van. He was the only man hurt, but it took several hours to get help."

Beth did not move. She stared into the warden's eyes until he looked down and rearranged a stack of documents and then absently drummed his fingers on the desktop for a moment. Beth waited for the warden to continue.

"What are you trying to tell me, sir? What has happened to my husband?"

He sat back and sucked in a lot of air before answering.

"He damaged his left leg badly. He has the use of both legs, but he has a little difficulty getting around. He uses a walking stick.

"I know this must be a shock, but we didn't inform you because your husband didn't wish you to be informed. He was quite insistent. He said you had never come to visit and that you were not to know about the accident. We all thought…we all thought he would tell you if you were still together."

She stood and held up her hand, so he warden would stop talking.

"When can I see my husband?"

"I can have him brought here now, if you like."

"Please. It's been a long time." The warden left through a door behind his desk, and Beth was left alone. *What will I say to him?*

The assistant warden returned through the same door almost immediately. "Mrs. Cross. He's here, but sometimes we need to prepare loved ones. He may not be the same man you knew before."

Beth nodded, but she was thinking back over the last six years and the six years before that and the six years before that. She remembered his firm hand with horses, his gentleness toward her, and his pride in Grady. She remembered all the bulls he'd ridden, and the dark fear that swept over her each time he nodded his head and another monster spun chaotically out of the chute with her husband clinging to its back. She knew he'd been bucked off, like all bull riders, but she did not remember even one time when he failed to ride the full eight seconds.

"Mrs. Cross?"

"No," she said firmly. "We'll be fine. He's still the same man."

"It's been six years, Mrs. Cross."

"I know what he was like when he was sent here. He hasn't changed."

***

Back before Grady was born, his mother and father drove north from Benton City, through the Hanford Reservation to the Vernita Bridge on the way to a rodeo in Othello. They stopped at Vernita to eat a quiet picnic on the river shore along the Hanford Reach, where the Columbia River flows as freely as it had at the time of Lewis and Clark. Upstream and downriver, the Columbia deepened and ran wide, slow, and warm behind the dams. But along the Hanford Reach, long-billed birds, elk, occasional beaver, and the salmon that ran deep through the region's heart were still present, if not plentiful.

The reactors were visible downstream, so Beth and Grady Sr. walked about a half a mile upstream to a quiet spot out of sight of the highway, the bridge, and the reactors. They spread an old blanket on the sandy ground and rested. She took off her shoes and waded up to her white ankles in the shallow water. He removed his boots. He stretched out on the sandy bank and stared at the white cliffs across the river to the north. She remembered this as one of the best days of their life together.

"We can't stay long, girl," Grady Sr. said. "I got a bull to ride. I got a good draw, and we need the money."

The young woman nodded but said nothing. She walked out of the river and lay down beside her young husband. He put both arms around her, and she rested her head on his shoulder.

"Why can't it be like this all the time?" she asked. "Quiet. Calm and peaceful. Do you think folks used to live like this all the time? Just restin' by the river. I could wash up every day in the cool water. You could rest a while, we could—"

"I got a bull to ride tonight. We need the money."

Later that afternoon in Othello, Grady Sr. did have a good bull. Too good. When he hit the ground awkwardly after two quick jumps, Beth sighed. He was in a slump and hadn't won a check in several weeks. She remembered what her husband said at the river.

"We need the money."

She got up to leave, but down in the arena, her husband was still on the ground on his hands and knees. He finally got up and moved toward the open chute, but he was moving much more slowly than usual. Beth watched until she was certain he could climb out of the arena under his own power and then made her way around the arena to where the truck was parked.

"I'll guess we'll go home and figure something out," she said aloud.

She was surprised to find her husband already at the truck when she arrived. He'd come directly from the arena without removing any of his gear. His protective vest was unzipped, and he was working on the tape that held his riding glove in place while he talked to an older man she recognized sitting on the truck's lowered tailgate. When Grady Sr. got the tape removed from his wrist, he tossed it and the glove into the truck bed. He did the same with his black hat. Beth knew he habitually left his chaps and vest on after an unsuccessful ride. When he stayed on for the full eight seconds, which nearly always meant he'd won a check, she would meet him at the truck, and his chaps, vest, gloves, and bull rope would already be neatly packed away in his riggin' bag. When he got bucked off, he never stayed behind the bucking chutes for the inevitable post-mortem small talk with the other bull riders. He returned to the truck to remove his gear and pack up alone.

Beth stopped. With one hand on the passenger-side door handle, she watched the two men talk. When they were through, the older man used both hands to propel himself down from the tailgate. Grady Sr. nodded and shook the man's hand. He glanced up at his wife then shrugged out of his vest and worked the straps of his chaps loose from the back of his legs. He unbuckled his chaps at the waist and folded them neatly on top of his vest. Then he carefully packed his gear into his riggin' bag. His folded chaps went in first. Then the vest. Next, he coiled his bull rope and placed it on top of the vest. He tucked in his leather riding glove last, zipped the bag closed, and moved it to the front of the truck bed, just behind the driver's seat. He shrugged his shoulders to the front and back several times to relieve an awkward pain and tightness he'd discovered between his shoulder blades.

He climbed into the truck and started the engine. He waited for his wife to pull herself up into her place in the passenger seat.

"I ain't goin' to be ridin' for a while," he said.

"What is it?" Beth asked. "Are you hurt?" She knew he was not inclined to let anyone know when he got hurt.

"No. Not so much. I landed kinda sideways, and my neck is tight and both shoulders is a little sore, but nothin' special."

She waited. He'd get around to telling her what he had on his mind.

"I got to go to Omak. That feller back there was Jed Knotts."

"I know Jed."

"He's got some work for me. Buncha his cows back in the canyons need to be brought down to the home place, and he's got some hay to get in. Had a young hotshot workin' for him, high school kid, but he took off to Montana with his rope horse and the work ain't gettin' done."

"You want to take me home first?"

"What do you want? Jed says we can stay in the house with him and his wife. Their kids is all gone."

"You know where I'd like to be."

"I'd like you to come along. It might be a' coupla months' work and Jed pays good."

"Okay then. Maybe I can help out some."

"Probably so. And after what that bull did to me, we surely do need the money."

***

The assistant warden left the room. When he returned, almost immediately, he pushed the office door open and stepped back. Grady Sr. hobbled through the door, leaning with his left arm on a heavy wooden cane. The warden left the room and closed the door softly behind him. Beth stood and turned to face her husband. She deliberately did not look at his legs.

"Well, I see you got yourself hurt. I guess you're going to have to stay home for a while now. Just until you heal up good."

Grady Sr. did not move. Despite his damaged leg, he stood erect, firm. "I reckon you can find somethin' useful for me to do around the place."

Tears were trying to form, but Beth squeezed her eyes shut so the tears would recede. She walked around the desk to her husband and touched his face. Her glistening eyes gazed into his, which were still hard and clear and icy blue, but a little moist. She felt she might disappear into that deep blue gulf.

CHAPTER 13

The Washington State Penitentiary at Walla Walla sat on the edge of the rolling Palouse wheat country and the spreading, rural suburbs of one of the oldest cities in that part of the country. Walla Walla, almost due east and a bit south of Grady's home in Richland, was being settled at about the same time as Seattle, the Pacific Northwest's regional capital nearly three hundred miles and a world away on the west side of the state.

After she met with her husband in the assistant warden's office. Beth returned to Richland, anxious to let Grady know his father would be home soon. Grady was unaware of exactly where his father had been for the last six years, so she did not know what kind of reaction to expect from her son. The boy had been sent away to Spokane to stay with Beth's sister during the trial and had not come home by the time Grady Sr. was taken to Walla Walla to begin his sentence. Grady had been only 12 when his father was sent away.

"Grady, son," Beth had said when she went to her sister's home to fetch him. "Your daddy won't be home when we get back."

"I know, mom," Grady shrugged and looked away. "It's okay."

"I don't know for sure when he'll be coming home. I don't know for sure if …" Grady was nearly as tall as mother by then. Beth put both of her hands on the boy's shoulders and turned him to face her.

"I know." Grady looked up at his mother. "I said it's okay." But Grady's chest began to heave and there were tears running down the boy's cheeks. Later, on the morning of the same day Grady was to ride a bull at the Pendleton Round-up, as she sat in the assistant warden's office waiting for her husband to be released, it would occur to Beth that was the last time she had seen Grady cry.

Grady Sr. made his own difficult way to the car, escorted by the assistant warden and two guards, professionals accustomed to dealing with hard cases, but who'd also become experts at recognizing men who no longer belonged behind Walla Walla's high walls and razor wire.

"You take care now," one of the guards said, a tall man with broad shoulders and hard eyes, after he had put a small bag containing Grady Sr.'s few belongings in the backseat of the car. He shook hands with Grady Sr. then stepped away. "I'd like to see that boy of yours rodeo one day."

"Me too."

The other guard, a shorter man with a close-cropped Marine haircut, helped Grady Sr. into the front passenger seat of the car. Beth was already in the driver's seat. He rolled down the window and said, "See ya 'round, boys, but I don't 'spect it'll be back here."

The assistant warden stepped forward and handed him a thick envelope. "You know the conditions of your release. You are unsupervised, but for a period of one year you must contact local law enforcement whenever you change residences. Good luck."

The second guard tapped the roof of the car lightly. Beth drove out of the prison and away from Walla Walla to the south.

"Just drive for a time," Grady Sr. said. "I want to see some countryside for a change."

Because they were in no hurry and because Grady Sr. wanted to see as little human activity as possible, Beth drove her husband away from the prison on back roads to the south, toward Milton-Freewater on the Oregon border. By September the wheat fields around Walla Walla had turned from deep green to rich golden brown. The weather in the previous twelve months had been nearly perfect—the right amount of moisture from adequate rain and winter snow and then a warm, dry summer. Here and there enormous combines worked around the clock harvesting the last of that year's abundance.

Beth kept silent. The car passed through Milton-Freewater at the Oregon border and headed into the open country past a road sign that read "Pendleton 34 Miles."

"Do you remember the last time we made this drive?" she asked.

"Yes, I do. Grady musta been six or seven. I'd done some harvest work for a guy in Milton-Freewater."

"Yes. It was twelve years ago this week. That farmer's wife had me and Grady come up to the house while you worked. I remember there were two big ol' shade trees in the yard and a creek running behind the house. Grady spent most of every day playing in that creek. You and the farmer washed off in the creek when the work was done."

Grady Sr. closed his eyes. "Yeah, I remember. After work me and you sat on the bank with our feet in the water. That was some hot work. I don't think water ever felt so good as it did washin' up on those hot days. Those was good times."

She stared straight ahead. The road toward Pendleton sloped gently through the brown countryside. No traffic at all, so she drove slowly.

"Grady's a good boy," she said. "You'll be proud of him."

"In your letters, you said Grady didn't finish school. Every day in prison it seems like someone'd be tellin' me I got to get more school. They sent me to classes inside, said I needed skills. Said that I couldn't ride bulls no more. I never thought it was true until the accident. So, I worked hard. This envelope's got a list of folks who might give me a job. But I can't seem to see past this here day or this here minute just yet."

Outside the car the road climbed steadily above the wheat fields. Beth pulled off the road and into a small, grassy park next to a hilltop cemetery. She turned off the engine, got out, and walked around the front of the car to help her husband get out. He held her shoulder for balance until he got his cane adjusted then moved awkwardly under his own power to a picnic table near the sagging fence that separated the park from the old graveyard.

They sat quietly. Below the park a vast wheat field swept up the sides of a narrow valley and glistened golden in the mid-morning sun. The road was visible at the bottom of the valley before it climbed sharply up the other side and disappeared over the top of the next hill. The park commanded a full view of the endless wheat stretching away golden in every direction. Two combines could be seen in the distance, one disappeared over the top of a hill to the west as the other became visible as it crested a similar hill on the other side of the valley. The combine to the east worked slowly in their direction through a cottony cloud of crop dust. The day was becoming warm, but in September the morning air held a hint of winter, so the breeze that drifted across the close-cut green grass of the graveyard was cool enough to cause her to tremble slightly. She moved closer to her husband and took his hand. Her delicate touch caused some of the ache in his damaged leg to melt away for a moment. She put a hand on his chin and turned his head toward her until she met and held his eyes.

"They'll be good times again," she said.

Grady Sr. did not move. The ache of incarceration had dulled his emotions. He felt no affection…only relief. He had developed a habit of living moment to moment, day to day, week to week. Good times? Not yet. Only time passing tolerably, meticulous and static.

"I got to get used to time moving again," he said. "I got to get my mind around to the idea that tomorrow matters."

"Our life's been on hold too," she said. "We been waitin' just like you have. Me and Grady waited while you was on all those long rodeo trips. Days, weeks. Months a couple a' times. The times you was home were good times. But when you were gone, we waited. Six years this time."

"I've thought about the times I was gone. I thought about it every day. I wish I had all those days on the road back again. I'd a' done better."

Grady Sr. turned away and gazed at the distant countryside beyond the old cemetery. He stood up and limped toward the graves. He scanned the names and dates on the crumbling tombstones just beyond the sagging fence. He thought about the lives lived. Love and hate. Joy and pain. Work and rest. Time together and time apart. What did those names and those dates add up to while each man or woman or child was alive, and what had been subtracted when each died?

"We've been waiting six years."

"I'd a' done better."

"I know. You will."

She stood and joined her husband at the graveyard fence.

"There's more than one way to be in prison. There's bein' locked out," she said. "There's more than one kind of punishment. If only I could have come to visit. If only you'd have let me visit."

"You wouldn't a' known me in there."

The breeze had stopped, and the sun warmed his shoulders. He looked away from his wife again. Beth returned to the table and stopped to stare into the valley with her back to him. A chill passed through her, and she wrapped her arms around her body. Suddenly, he was at her side. She did not turn in his direction.

"Those six years is gone now," she spoke softly. "It seems like you only been away for a little while, like on a rodeo trip. It's been hard for me and the boy. But right now, in this little, quiet place with everythin' good spread out below us, it seems like all that time don't matter at all, like those years are buried here in this graveyard. Having you here is like we've all come back to life, and it was only time that was lost. How could so much hard living get jammed into a time that doesn't seem all that big anymore?"

The breeze returned, warm this time.

Leaning heavily on his cane, he used his free arm to turn her toward him. He stroked her cheek. She took his hand in both of hers and pulled it to her lips.

"We're free now," she said. "We're not waiting any more. The time has come to get moving." She helped her husband get back in the car. And they drove together down into the valley and on over the hill toward Pendleton.

***

Pendleton, Oregon sat at the bottom of a steep canyon with the Umatilla River at the bottom. The motel where Grady and Jill stayed was on the flat southeastern rim of the canyon. On the morning he was scheduled to ride his bull at the Pendleton Round-Up, they drove past the hundred-year-old Olney Cemetery and took a right on the steep decline of Southgate Avenue. Grady could see the grandstands of the Pendleton Round-Up grounds off to the left. He turned left at the bottom of the hill, drove three blocks west, and pulled the truck into a gate marked "Competitors Only." He gave the attendant his name, and the man at the gate reminded Grady to check with the secretary at the rodeo office then waved him through the gate. Grady found a place to park the truck in a long row of mostly newer rigs in the gravel lot behind the north grandstands near the stock pens and several dozen colorful Native American tepees.

Without a word to Jill, he got out of the truck and headed toward the stock pens to have a look at the bulls. He was up in the first performance later that afternoon and would need to check with the secretary to see which bull he had drawn, but first he wanted to see the bulls. Jill was surprised by Grady's abrupt exit from the truck, so she followed him at what seemed like a safe distance.

When she caught up, Grady was standing a few feet back from the steel panels that formed the stock pens. The first pen held twelve bulls. She was a little surprised that the bulls were not all the same size and that each had distinctive markings and that not all had horns. She thought bulls always had horns. She stopped a few feet behind Grady and said nothing. When she moved up next to him, she asked, "Which one are you going to ride?" The boy did not answer immediately.

"I don't know yet."

"Have you ever ridden any of these bulls before?"

Again, he did not answer right away. Then he said, "That black one, there, with the horns that turn down, like a banana. I almost won a big check on him at the Bull-O-Rama in Ellensburg. He nearly did me some serious damage, though. The bull fighter jumped in and got him away, just in time."

"Just in time?"

"Yeah. But that's the way it always seems to be. Just when you think the bull's about to get you, the bullfighter jumps in. When they're late, it can be bad for the bull rider. But the good ones aren't late."

"This is awful dangerous, isn't it, Grady?"

Grady was silent. Like all rodeo folks, he had known bull riders who had been hurt badly. Half the old timers he knew, including Hazard Quinn, walked with a limp. Even those who didn't had some part of their body that hurt most of the time. Grady didn't say so, but he'd known two boys, one younger than him, who had been killed riding bulls. Still, even knowing all that, he had by necessity pushed an awareness of the danger down into a deep place beneath all other emotion and against all reason.

"No one thinks about it. Can't."

She took two slow steps in front of him and put both hands on the second rail of the pen. The bull that had bucked Grady off in Ellensburg took two steps toward Jill and snorted. The beast lowered his head and threw dirt back into the air, first with its right front hoof then with the left. Startled, she stepped back and bumped into Grady. She quickly took an awkward half step to the right then turned back toward him.

"You ever been hurt?"

"Riding bulls? Not bad. I been stepped on a few times, kicked hard once, but I've been lucky, I guess. Luckier than some. I guess my time'll come."

"Then why do it?"

"I guess it don't matter much why. I just do it. I've never really learned to do much else. I guess why don't matter that much. I been goin' to rodeos since I was little. All us kids would run around the rodeo grounds playing cowboy. We'd climb on the chutes and run around the stock pens like it weren't nothin'. Sometimes we'd even sit up on the fence and try to rope the bulls with our little toy ropes. The moms would tell us to be careful, and we'd say 'we will' then go do what we wanted. The dads mostly let us run around and play."

He walked forward and leaned on the top rail of the pen. The bull snorted again then took one careful step in his direction. Grady did not move.

"We saw guys get hurt rodeoin' all the time. But it weren't nothin' to us. It's the way things are."

Jill stepped up and stood next to Grady, and the bull backed off a step when she did.

"I still don't understand," she said quietly. "I don't want you to get hurt."

"My mom says that to me every time I head out to rodeo. I 'spect she said the same thing to my dad when he was still around."

"I guess to her there's no difference."

"There's a difference. My mom went to every one of my dad's rodeos she could. She went to all my rodeos when I was little. But she ain't seen me ride once since my dad left."

"Why?"

"I don't really know. I guess it don't matter much if anyone's there when I ride or not."

His response surprised Jill. She turned away and stared at the black bull. His head was down, and his nostrils were flaring.

"Oh yes, it does matter." She turned away quickly and headed back toward John's truck.

Her sudden departure caught Grady by surprise. "I got to check on my draw and pay my fees," he said, but she was already gone.

Jill did not stop. She continued on away from his voice. When she reached the truck, she climbed into the driver's seat where

Grady had sat on the drive to Pendleton. The familiar tug had returned, and she covered her face with her hands.

***

The morning Grady and Jill drove from Joseph to Pendleton, the Lower Yakima Valley was bright and sunny, but a thick bank of moisture was pushing its way up from the Columbia thirty miles to the south. Frank had returned to the ranch with another load of hay on a flatbed trailer. He parked his pickup and the trailer next to the barn. John came out of the house, and Frank got out of the truck.

"Go on in and get some coffee," John said. "I'll back the trailer up next to the stack and we can unload after you've had somethin' to eat."

Frank went through the back door of the house, hung his coat on a hook in the mudroom, and went into the kitchen. Adah was standing at the stove.

"Have some coffee and sit down," she said. "I'll have somethin' for you to eat in a minute."

"You don't have to make nothin' for me. Coffee's enough."

"Suit yourself. There's stew here on the stove and bread in the oven if you want it." Adah pulled her chair from its place next to the stove. She sat down and slowly lifted each leg onto the footrests.

Frank ignored her. He took a large mug from the drainer next to the sink and filled it with coffee from the ancient percolator on the stove. He leaned against the counter near the sink and took a careful two-handed sip. Adah sat up straight and looked at Frank who did not move. He took another sip from his mug as he turned to glance out the window. In the distance he could barely see the rise of the Horse Heaven Hills, which were shrouded in a heavy mist gliding down the northern face. When it reached the valley floor, the mist would join the morning moisture from the Yakima River and become a dense fog that would slow traffic on the interstate just above the river.

"There's going to be fog in the valley later," he said. "Maybe I'd better stay out here in case John needs help."

"That'd be fine."

"The weather ain't going to turn cold for a while, but I think you might get some more rain out here in the next couple a' days. It might be best for me to stay."

"If you think so," Adah said. "Then you should stay. John likes to have you around to help out."

"Yeah, it might be best."

The mist reached the base of the hills, and Frank watched through the kitchen window as it began to obscure first the highway and then the valley floor. The fog dropped over the edge of the riverbank and into the Yakima River, hovered there, and began to creep up the gentle slope of the north bank. He remained silent, and Adah did not move.

"Okay, then," he said after a while. He took a step toward the door to the mudroom. "I'll go help unload that hay."

"There'll be time for that in a while. Let's us talk."

"What you want to talk about?" He stopped and leaned back against the sink again. They remained silent for a while.

"Frank, you been avoidin' that boy that's been stayin' here. Don't seem like you should have any hard feelins toward him."

"His daddy killed my brother."

"Well, there's that, I 'spect. But I don't understand why you're holdin' hard feelings against Grady. He was a child when it happened.

He twirled the mug in both hands. He sat it carefully on the counter next to the sink.

"The boy is here now," Adah said. "Maybe it's time. The time weren't quite right before."

"Time for what? Time is passed all these years and nothin's changed."

"Yes, son. Your brother's gone. Been gone a long time. Goin' to stay gone. That boy's daddy's been gone a long time."

"That's right. And he should stay gone," he said in angry whisper. "I was there, old woman. I saw my brother die."

She softened her voice. "Think how hard it is for that boy to live with this. You lost a brother, and there ain't no hope for that. Grady's lost his daddy, but that ain't hopeless. You got to forgive yourself. And you got to forgive that boy and his daddy."

He retrieved his mug from the counter next to the sink. He refilled it from the pot on the stove and turned back toward the kitchen window. The fog reached the valley floor, crossed the river, and continued to roll up the northern bank. If the wind remained calm, the fog would billow into a great earthbound cloud before it leveled out up the slope toward John's place. Adah placed both hands on the arms of her chair, pushed herself onto her feet, and took two stiff steps toward Frank who was still staring out the window. She stopped behind him, so she could see the fog rolling back on itself in the near distance. She reached up and placed a hand on his right shoulder and turned him toward her. He dropped his eyes.

"That boy ain't even had hope to live with all this time," she said. "That boy is lost. Until he knows you and John have let this go, he ain't goin' to see nothin' but trouble."

Frank raised his head slightly, and she brushed his cheek with her fingertips.

"He's tryin' to become a man. The truth ain't goin' to change, so you got to change. Unless you do and unless you tell Grady you have, he won't be no kind a' man at all."

"Adah, I ain't goin' to do that. I can't." His voice faltered. "That boy don't need nothin from me. Time has passed. The boy must a' got over losing his daddy by now. Time heals…"

She tapped his chin hard. Startled, he tried to look away, but she had moved her hands to each side of his face. She stared up at him and held his attention with a gaze that burned through his confusion and into the hard, clear core of the profane fact that he'd been hiding from all his life.

"Time don't do nothin' but pass by. It don't change nothin'. The truth is the truth, and ain't no one, not you or me or John or that boy can change it. Time passin' ain't goin' to change it. All we can do is say it when we know what it is. And what we know is that you got to let this thing go."

He took hold of Adah's wrist and firmly pulled her hands away from his face. He walked to the mudroom and shrugged into his coat. He stomped out of the house and went out to help John unload and stack the hay.

***

Early the next morning, a bright Wednesday the second week in September, Adah surprised Anne by pushing the door to her room open with her foot. She sat erect in her chair, and Anne was stunned by how tall she looked. In turn Adah was surprised by how much more worried and haggard Anne looked every day.

"John's thinks Grady and Jill will be in Pendleton for the rodeo today. We're all goin'. Me and John and Frank. I figured you'd want to come along."

"You think they'll be at the rodeo?"

"Makes sense. Grady told John he was up the first day at Pendleton. That's today, so we're all going down there to see what we can see. I reckon we'll find 'em there."

Adah turned her chair away from the door and wheeled down the hall. Anne got off the bed and walked out of the room and followed Adah down the hall to the kitchen.

"Of course, I'm going! I've been worried sick. When are we leaving?"

"Soon as you're dressed and ready. You can gulp some coffee and there's some biscuits left to eat on the way if you want. And there ain't no point worryin' about that girl. Whatever's goin' to happen has already happened."

"Adah, please. You're not helping."

"Don't mean to be helpin'. Get ready to go. Frank and John's waitin'."

CHAPTER 14

nd that was how Anne came to sit in the backseat of Frank's truck. Frank was driving and appeared to be brooding, his shoulders drooped, and his eyes locked onto the road, with John in the front passenger seat. Adah was in the back behind Frank with Anne on the passenger side. They drove through the rolling wheat fields south of Kennewick toward the Columbia River and Oregon. The arid hills rolled away from the highway on each side of the truck. A stiff wind stirred up dust as they passed broad swaths of summer fallow, plowed ground left bare, so the soil would replenish itself. The earthy, sweet smell of newly cut wheat blew in through the open windows.

***

Jill was still asleep when Grady left the motel to check his riggin' bag. He set the bag on the flat bed of John's truck. He began by examining his bull rope for worn spots. He always packed an extra leather glove to wear on his right hand, the hand the bull rope would be wrapped around when it came time to nod himself out of the chute. He rubbed the palm of his riding glove and worked the leather in each finger to make sure it was still supple. He checked the stitching at the wrist. He also made sure he had the worn glove his father had left. The old leather was dry and cracked, and Grady wasn't sure he'd ever seen his father wear it. He found it one night buried in a box of his father's old gear, which his mother was about to throw out. He took his father's glove with him every time he traveled to a rodeo. He packed the old glove in the bottom of his bag with his chaps, bull rope, and his good gloves on top. He zipped the riggin' bag closed, slung it over his shoulder, and went outside to put the bag in John's truck. This was not the last time he would check his gear.

It was still half dark when he hefted his bag into the backseat of John's truck. He placed both hands on top of the bag and went once more down a mental checklist to make sure he had everything. Then he leaned against the front fender to watch the sun come up. He reached both arms over his head with his hands clasped and leaned back against the front fender to stretch the long muscles in his chest and torso. Then he spread his feet apart and let his upper body fall forward to stretch his lower back and the tight muscles in the back of his legs. When he felt the edginess begin to abate, he stood up and stared out across the countryside. He squinted when the sunlight reached his face and shaded his eyes with his right hand. After a few moments, his eyes began to adjust to the light and his mind began to settle on what he had to do. He went back into the motel room to wake Jill for breakfast, thinking it was a good day to ride a bull.

✳✳✳

John had let Adah have her way when Grady and Jill left. It wasn't that he thought Jill was too young or that Grady was reckless. *Even if the boy did take advantage,* he thought. *It wouldn't be the first time such a thing had happened. Maybe he already had, and that's why the girl was so willing to run off with him.* He was relieved Jill would soon be reunited with her mother and was in an amiable mood.

Normally silent on a long drive, John started talking as soon as he got into the front passenger seat and didn't stop for the forty minutes it took the truck to work its way from his place to the freeway south of Kennewick.

"Ever been to a rodeo before?" he asked Anne. "A lot of folks around here take their kids to the big rodeo at the Kennewick Fair. Figure the kids need to see the rodeo at least once. The next year they take 'em to the car races and the next year to something else. Nothin' ain't never the same for some folks."

"Can't stand the things myself," Adah said. She did not like traveling and was agitated. "But young people and old timers seem to like 'em good enough. Too much dirt, too many cows, and too many cowboys tryin' to prove they got it, when mostly they ain't."

"But you got to go to the rodeo all the time to really see it," John said. "It ain't never the same twice. Sometimes a steer'll pull a headin' horse right over on his side. One time I saw a calf cut to the right in front of an ol' boy's horse, and the horse got tangled up with the calf and flipped over right on top of that cowboy. Looked like a bad wreck, but nothin' much happened to the horse or the cowboy. The horse got up, the cowboy got up, and everybody was alright. They was out there again the next weekend."

"Yeah," Adah chirped. "Lots a' fun. Perfect place for a young'un in Jill's state a mind."

Grady would not have appreciated the talk about wrecks on horses. To a "roughie", a bull rider or a guy who rode bucking horses, ropers were never in much real danger. Most people, who weren't rodeo folks, didn't go to the rodeo to see the ropers or even the ponytailed cowgirls on their agile barrel horses. Most people came to see the rough stock, the bucking horses and, especially, the bull riders. A roughie never thought much about the crowd, but he sometimes had a sense right before he got on a bucking horse or a bull that everyone in the stands had bought a ticket to see him get "throwd and stomped."

John started in again.

"One time up in Omak, they got some crazy Indian cowboys up there. Boys sure enough can ride, though. Well, I had a good seat with a friend on the rodeo committee.

"We were sittin' right next to the announcer, just about on top of the buckin' chutes, so you could look straight down and see the bulls get loaded and the cowboys get on. There was this one Indian kid, first time in a big rodeo, I heard later. He was scared plumb spitless. He stood behind the first chute and watched this big bull jump up and try to get his front legs over the end of the chute. I guess the bull thought he could climb out maybe. The bull could reach far enough up on the end of the chute so he could pull himself up.

"Well, they got that bull settled down and the cowboy, he goes to get on the bull and the critter makes one more big jump. Gets his front legs up over the end again and pulls himself up, so that he hits his mouth on the deck that's around the announcer's booth, which ain't high enough to be much outa the way. He breaks off some teeth and leaves them in a little pool of blood right there on the deck.

"The Indian kid he sees this, so's he's even scarder than he was before. He sorta backs away from that chute, and I think maybe he decides he's not goin' to be takin' part in the bull ridin' that day.

"Well, the boys, they get that bull necked up to the chute real good, and they call to the Indian kid to go ahead and get on, and danged if he doesn't climb right up over the top a' the chute and gets himself settled down on that bull. He pulls his rope up good 'n tight and is about to nod when that ol' bull jerks his head loose from the guys holding the neck rope and goes to buckin' right there in the chute.

"The kid, he's taken by surprise and gets throwd straight up, and he gets a toe of his boot caught up in the panel at the back of the chute and goes on over backwards. You can just about hear his knee pop as he goes over the back of the chute and lands hard on his back, right down below us.

"Well, it's right obvious to everyone that the kid is hurt bad, but he manages to get up on his feet, favoring that knee careful like. He hops around gentle fer a minute or two, checking to see that all the vital parts still worked. Well, I sit back and shake my head at my friend on the committee. Bad luck for that Indian kid to draw that bull. See, I'm thinkin' it's kinda sad, his first pro rodeo and he pays his fees and don't even get to ride.

"Then I sit up some and see that boy yellin' at the crew in the arena. He hops one-legged up on the back of the chute and climbs back down on that bull again. He pulls his rope up good 'n tight once more, takes a good tight wrap, sits up tall, nods his head, and that bull jumps outa the chute sideways and goes to buckin' and spinin' like his disposition hadn't improved none.

"That kid, he nearly loses his seat on the first jump, but then he settles in and is workin' with that bull like nothin' you never saw in your life. The buzzer rings in loud and that young Indian kid just keeps a ridin'. Finally, the bull gets the better of him, and after about fifteen seconds, the boy comes un-seated and is pitched over the front of the bull. The critter lowers his head like he's goin' to kill that boy, but the bullfighters jump in like they always do and get the bull away. The cowboy ain't movin' at all, but we can see he's breathin', and then he sits up. He waves his hat to the crowd.

I never heard no bunch a' rodeo folks cheer so long or so loud for nothin' in my life."

Even with the windows down, the cab of the old truck was hot and stuffy in the mid-morning heat. The air cooled when they crossed the Columbia River Bridge at Umatilla, Oregon. To their left the spillways of the McNary Dam were open to allow excess water rushing down from Canada and from the Snake River Watershed as far away as Wyoming to tumble toward the Pacific Ocean.

At Umatilla the Columbia straightened out for its final two-hundred-mile run to the Pacific. McNary Dam was at the extreme downriver end of a thirty-mile bend in the river that began upstream at Walulla Gap.

"Want to stop at the dam and see the fish in the ladders?" John asked. "This time of year, the fish ladders ought to be pretty well full."

"Stop? No. We've got to find Jill," Anne said.

He waited.

"No one wants to see fish," Adah said.

"Well," he said. "Guess we ought to get on down to Pendleton. Maybe on the way back."

Frank drove on another ten miles before he hit Interstate 84 and turned southeast toward Pendleton. He scrunched over against the driver's side door and remained silent, driving with one hand. Anne noticed the countryside here was a lot like the land around John's place, only flatter and bigger somehow. The landscape rolled swiftly away from the river to the south toward the vast wilderness of eastern Oregon and to the west toward the urban waste of Portland. In the distance to the east, she could see the beginnings of the Blue Mountains.

"Is that where Jill and Grady went?" Anne asked, pointing across the front seat toward the mountains.

"I reckon so," Adah said.

"What's up there?"

Frank sat up and pushed hard against the steering wheel with both hands. Anne could feel the front seat move.

"Nothin'," he said. He leaned forward and pressed down on the accelerator. The truck sped up dramatically, and in twenty minutes, they were racing down a steep hill and into Pendleton.

CHAPTER 15

Grady Sr. hadn't been thinking about where they were headed. He was content sit back and watch the open countryside. As they came into Pendleton from the northeast, it hit him.

"What day is it?" he said.

"Wednesday."

"It's round-up week. The Pendleton Round-Up starts today."

"Yes. I know."

"So, we're going to the rodeo? Is that why you came down here?"

"Your first day back and all, it's somewhere to go."

"I don't know. The only cows I've seen the last six years were in the prison dairy."

"Grady's up today. He's goin' to ride a bull in the Round-up."

Grady Sr. leaned back into his seat. "Really? The bulls is tough at Pendleton. You told me he'd been ridin', but you never said how he'd been doin'."

"You never asked. Seemed like you didn't want to know nothin' about what was going on with me and Grady."

He ran his fingers up and down his cheek. The rough stubble reminded him that he had not shaved and called to mind the regimentation of the last six years when even everyday tasks were scheduled. He looked out the passenger-side window at the broad expanse as the last wheat field gave way to intermittent small farms.

"I couldn't stand to know. When you first go in, the old timers say you got to make time stop. But it don't stop. I lived every day and felt every minute I was there. I knew Grady would grow up and I wouldn't be around. I could imagine 'im growin' up, but not seein' it, not knowin' it... not bein' there to show him how."

"He's won some money," Beth said. "And he hasn't been hurt, so I guess he's been doin' okay."

Grady Sr. had ridden bulls at the Pendleton Round-Up. He never won, but in his second year on the circuit, he made it to the short go, the Saturday performance when the top cowboys and cowgirls in each event ride and rope for the really big checks.

"I remember a bull I got on down here," he said. Long time ago. Thought I had 'im rode, but I got to showin' off. Spurred 'im once or twice, tryin' to pick up an extra point or two. He stopped sudden and changed directions. I ended up on the ground. Would of been the biggest check I ever won."

"You ended up under that bull."

He rubbed his cheek again.

"That's the closest I ever come to gettin' killed."

"I know that."

As they drove into town past the Pendleton Woolen Mills, State Highway 11 became Court Street, then Dorian, which crossed Main Street at the center of town.

"Park over by the train station," he said. "We can walk down Main Street, then along the river to the rodeo grounds."

Beth parked the car, and they strolled down Main Street toward the Umatilla River. Grady Sr. moved with greater ease. He leaned on the cane only occasionally now. Main Street was always closed during round-up week, jammed with food vendors selling everything from Native American fry bread to German sausages and teriyaki chicken, all set up in the middle of the street. Leather goods, Western hats and boots, belt buckles, and Pendleton Round-Up tee shirts and caps were all available. At the corner of Main and Court, with Hamley's Saddlery on the right, they walked on for one more block before they reached the paved path that followed the river to the round-up grounds.

***

John leaned against a corral panel behind the main grandstand and watched the bulls loaf calmly. He let his eyes follow the slope above the houses to the tree line and then to the sky. He noticed the town had inched higher up the slopes of the canyon than he remembered, but he also knew that to the south and east the rigidly contained city gave way to a wilderness that hadn't changed since the time when miners and settlers and the Nez Perce Indians fought a war over it.

"I coulda lived up in them mountains," he said softly. "In another time, maybe."

He was often wistful in such moments. A man in his profession spends much of his time alone, seldom still, but often alone. While on horseback in search of wayward cattle or on foot mending endless fences, straining to keep excess civilization at a safe distance, John often sought illumination from his recent past, backlit by his indistinct earlier history.

His first wife had given him three hard-born sons and fifteen years of endless grief. The woman's inevitable departure produced both sadness and relief. Without the moderating influence of a stubborn woman, John allowed his sons to grow up in a household defined by male pursuits, including a long procession of "girlfriends," not all of whom had been single. The boys also had easy access to booze. He was haunted by the notion that his sons might be a reflection of the life he lived in those days. His children were already grown and perfectly suited to their father's way of living, before he knew what they needed from him.

The middle son, Robert, lived a life with little connection to John or Frank somewhere in the mountains around Boise, Idaho. John had not seen him since Charlie was killed. Frank stayed close, but John could see that his oldest son had been changed by the death of his brother. Frank did what was required of him but had also become prone to long periods of brooding punctuated by heavy drinking and outbursts of almost homicidal violence. He had been jailed twice after fights with young men who had been friends. As a result, his circle of acquaintances had gradually diminished. Occasionally, he filled his days with temporary work for farmers and ranchers up and down the Yakima Valley, and he frequently filled his nights with aimless wandering behind the wheel of his pickup.

John's own response to Charlie's death had been predictable. When Frank brought the news home and explained what had happened, John was immediately possessed by a consuming rage and a profound hatred for the man who had killed his son. Then he was consumed by an almost suicidal disappointment in his own failure neither to protect the boy nor to teach him to govern his demons. During the trial in Yakima, aborted after two days when the killer confessed in order to secure a shorter prison sentence, John sat in the first row of seats and never took his eyes off the man who had killed his son. Strangely, neither John's anger, nor his firm and determined hatred, nor even an awareness of his own failure, ever turned to grief. He was pleased when the killer was sent to prison, and he secretly promised himself he would make things right whenever the man was released. He would take the man's life.

One year to the day after Charlie's death, Adah rescued John. She was older, though how much older, he never knew for sure, and he never asked. Like all women of a certain age, it was hard to tell whether Adah had been a beauty when she was younger, at least outwardly. But by the time John had met her, she'd gained the certainty older people often accomplish when time, squeezed by the diminishing years, speeds up and the future becomes tangible and visible.

On the day he met Adah, John was slumped on the curb in front of the only tavern on the main street of Benton City on a warm Fourth of July afternoon. In a park not far from the tavern, he heard church music, high-pitched singing. "Bringing In the Sheaves." This was not an oddity in an old town like Benton City, which recognized neither the temptation nor the compulsion to dwell in the present. John had no objection to the music, but he was hung over, and the singing did nothing to ease the throbbing between his temples.

After a few moments, the music stopped. John watched a few locals set up barricades for the Independence Day parade. People began to wander out of the park and down the street past John as he teetered on the curb with his knees bent and his feet in the gutter. Stoic patriarchs led family groups, and hopeful grandmothers advanced up the street despite their infirmities. Youngsters rode above it all on their fathers' shoulders or bounced along on a mother's hip. And couples of every age walked arm in arm. Everyone seemed to be with someone else.

The small crowd had nearly passed him by when John became aware of a presence behind him. He twisted his head around without getting up, and there was Adah, standing over him, leaning on a wooden walking stick. John squinted at her and started to get up, but his head began to throb again, so he settled back down and turned away. Adah spoke to John from behind and from above, like the impatient voice of God speaking truth to the prodigal.

"Well, sir, I guess you're just about all the way into the gutter there, ain't you?"

John turned around again, this time in the other direction. His head didn't hurt quite so much, so he pushed himself to his feet and faced Adah. She was still several inches shorter than John even though she was standing erect on the sidewalk and he was slouching in the gutter.

"Excuse me…ma'am?"

"Well, now you're all the way in. I guess that finishes it."

"In where?"

"The gutter. Looks like you're pretty much all the way gone. So, I guess I'll be goin' somewhere where I can do some good."

"I'm standing in the street."

"The street, the gutter, it don't take no genius to see you're at a place no man wants to be."

He looked down. He *was* in the gutter along with street grime, dead leaves, a couple of crushed beer cans, and at least one rotting robin.

"I think I know who you are," Adah said. "Preacher here says there's a man lost his son about a year back and he'd let his place out in the country somewhere go completely to seed. Well, it sure looks like you're on your way, and that's a fact. You that man?"

"I don't see how it's none a' your business who I am or where I'm headed."

"You're right about that. Ain't none a' my concern. But I thought you might like to know that there's people who know you and want to see you take a turn, to go down a different road and get back home."

John looked at his feet again. A young man on the crew setting up barricades lifted the dead bird out of the gutter and put it in a garbage can. Adah had started up the street alone, following the crowd that had been in the park. John stepped up onto the sidewalk and took a step in her direction.

"Ma'am?" he said loud enough for Adah to hear.

She stopped and turned. She took a step back toward him. "We'll be back in the park again after the parade. Right along about sundown. Y'all come."

He watched Adah walk away slowly up the street. He felt very tired. He shuffled toward the curb to resume his seat with his feet in the gutter. The heat had increased, and he could feel sweat beginning to collect on the back of his neck and between his shoulder blades. Soon the back of his shirt would be soaked, and the tavern was air-conditioned. John knew just about everyone who was likely to be in the tavern this time of day, so there was a good chance he could get someone to buy him a beer. He'd spent all the money he'd brought to town in the same tavern the night before and had not returned home since.

He took his foot out of the gutter and glanced again in the direction Adah had gone. He got up and pulled on the tavern door.

Cold air rushed out followed by a dim kaleidoscope of beer signs, scratchy country music, and drunken laughter.

"Hey, John," someone inside yelled. "If you'll come on in and close the frickin' door, I'll buy you a cold one. Looks like you could use a little hair of the dog, son."

John did not answer. He stepped back and let the door close slowly. He felt cold all over, as if the refrigerated air of the tavern had settled in his bones. He shivered and became dizzy. His stomach began to cramp, and he lurched forward and put his hands on his knees. He thought he might throw up.

Still bent over, he took several awkward steps toward the street. When he reached the curb, he hung his head and stared down into the gutter. His vision cleared, and he could see the impression his feet had made in the street grime. He squeezed his eyes closed and began to step off the curb. When he opened his eyes, he was still on the sidewalk, but his vision had blurred again. He stumbled toward the park.

Most of the small towns in eastern Washington had a park somewhere in the vicinity of what passed for a central business district. In the more prosperous communities, which were generally found in wheat country, there would be a swimming pool and occasionally even a golf course. Benton City had neither. The park in Benton City was a mostly green, grassy rectangle, one block wide and a little more than two blocks long. A narrow alley ran between the park and the backside of a row of permanent businesses that faced Main Street, directly across from the tavern. The town's only bank anchored the south end of the block. Next were the hardware store and the cramped city hall. At the north end of the block, but still opposite the park, was the only two-story structure in town. The business space on the first floor changed occupants so often it was difficult for the townspeople to remember whether it was a pizza parlor, a daycare center, or a consignment shop. The second floor contained about a dozen very cheap and shabby one-room apartments. The tenants on the second floor sometimes included members of the town's small collection of eccentrics.

The park was flat on the north end and sloped up to the east on the southern end. At the bottom of the slope was a small, concrete square where a sound system could be set up. The square, nestled among several large shade trees and surrounded by picnic tables, sat directly in front of a large public kitchen that was open on the side facing the park. At public gatherings, people—in this case Adah's congregation—could lounge on the grass or sit at the picnic tables. When John arrived, the park was empty except for three or four families from Adah's group who had stayed behind to picnic before the parade.

John found a spot under a smaller tree away from the few families gathered at the shady south end of the park. He sat down with his back against the tree and closed his eyes to wait. About an hour later, he heard the parade pass by on Main Street. It did not last long, and as soon as it ended, people returned to the south end of the park. He stood up and leaned against the tree.

He could see a small stage had been erected on the concrete square and a man in a tight-fitting, black coat with a matching Stetson was about to speak. The man leaned into the microphone and mumbled something to the small crowd. John strained to hear what the man was saying, but everyone had risen at once and had begun to sing, without accompaniment and without doubt.

"Praise God from Whom all blessings flow…"

The melody was familiar to John, and the words of the first line seemed a vague memory from someplace deep down and long ago, as from a distant country where he had once lived. The voice of the congregation seemed to elevate on the second verse, and John pushed himself away from the tree and took several tentative steps in the direction of the small crowd.

"Praise Him, all creatures here below…"

The words came back to him. He mouthed the second line silently and then recited the third line in time with the music as he moved toward the edge of the gathering.

"Praise Him above, ye heavenly host…"

John was singing full out by the time he had reached the final line.

"Praise Father, Son, and Holy Ghost."

He held the final note a bit too long and was a bit embarrassed until he realized that no one had noticed. When the final line had been sung, the entire congregation sat, most on the grass, but some on park benches or at scattered picnic tables. All except the man at the microphone in the black hat. And all except John who stared across the crowd to where he could see Adah who was standing alone, nodding her head, and mouthing the words "Yes, Jesus."

CHAPTER 16

John thought a long time about what to do next. Then he pushed himself away from the corral panel and headed back toward the park.

It was there he saw a familiar couple sitting at another picnic table. *The boy's parents.* He stopped for a moment. He remembered the hate he'd felt toward this man six years before. He remembered his determination to end the man's life. He thought of young Grady deprived of a father. And he remembered the words Adah said to him on that Fourth of July evening, after he had poured out the story of his own dead son and of the other boy's father locked away in prison. Since that night, Adah had regularly repeated the same words to John. "You can't hate that man forever. You can only hate him 'til you die, and if you keep on hatin' him, you'll die soon, and you'll die forever."

As John watched Grady's parents, he searched deep, but found nothing of the hate that had been the only part of his self in the old days. "Those times are past," he said aloud.

He walked up to the picnic table where the man and the woman were sitting together facing John. Grady Sr. recognized John instantly. First fear and then anger shot up and down his spine and settled in his gut. He put both hands on the table and started to stand up.

"No," John said, gesturing with both hands that the man should remain seated. "Don't get up. I'm no threat to you. I just wonder if I could sit a spell."

John sat down across from Grady's parents and said, "I'd like to talk some about our boys."

✳✳✳

In the year or so after he met her, Adah convinced John that a man's entire obligation is to live his life out to its natural conclusion. The pain of losing a son would not pass quickly, she told him, and the anger would persist unless he could forgive the man responsible.

"John, you got to let him go. Or he's going to have a powerful grip on you."

Once, after they had been together a short time, Adah told him it wasn't what people have in common that keeps them together. More often it's the blank spaces in one that need to be filled in by the other.

"But first," she said. "You got to admit you got blank spots. The emptiness won't never close up, but someone else may be able to fill those places up with somethin' good. Or you may find somethin' way down inside yourself, somethin' you didn't even know was there, to fill up the empty spot."

John's blank spots were filled with disappointment, anger, and hate, which all added up to a profound unacknowledged and unfelt grief, and even shame. "That's the hold he's got on you," she said again. "Forgive him, and he'll let go. You'll be free."

Adah was small, and her body was weak. John was strong. Both had gleaned from a life of daily toil the hard truth that nothing comes easy, but that all things do come. John sank into a hole of bitterness when his son was killed. He was determined to do either himself or the man responsible as much harm as he could, because finally and for a long time, he held himself responsible for the death of his boy. John and Adah had complementary shortcomings, but she possessed a stubborn and practical optimism that escaped him at first, but which, ultimately, rescued him.

"When we've hit the bottom, we ain't got but two choices, and that is to climb back up or stay down and die," Adah told him. "When we almost get to where we was before, we got one more big step to take. We got to forgive, and we got to seek forgiveness.

"You can't hate no man forever, John. Not without comin' to hate yourself by and by. You got to get past this hurt and then go find the man that killed your son…and forgive 'im, right to his face."

"I can't forget, Adah," he said. "I can't. Death don't go away. There just ain't no reason to keep livin' in a world where such a thing could happen. I figure if I'm going to die, the man who did this is going to go with me."

"I ain't saying you should forget what happened. Ain't no such thing as forgivin' and forgettin'. There's only forgivin'. You're hatin' two men right now. You got to let both hates go. That's the only way you'll get back on your feet and outa that gutter. There's no other way to bring that dead spot back to life, you got to fill it up with love for that man and pity for what you've both had to live with. Otherwise, the rest of you is goin' to die, and soon."

John sat down at the table while Grady Sr. remained standing with his wife's hand on his arm. She gripped his shirtsleeve.

"Sit down," she said. "Let's see what this man has to say."

Grady Sr. sat down next to his wife. He was tense. The relief he had felt at being released from prison was gone. He was suddenly aware of a great, unwalled expanse opening up around him. He felt a fear and a thrill that had been buried for all those years.

"Inside, in prison, time is all closed up," he said. "It's best not to expect much. There's no truth inside, at least there's no place to stand on what a man knows. I know you got cause to hate me. And I know I didn't mean your boy no harm. I didn't know he was hurt so bad. I swear, and that's why I—"

John held up his hand. "I don't need to hear nothin' from you. Time's passed. Ain't much good's come out of all this so far's I can see."

Beth released her grip on her husband's shirt and moved her hand to gently rub the muscles of his upper arm. She looked at John and said, "We've come to see our son. Our Grady's in the bull riding here today. They haven't seen each other in more'n six years. I'm not right sure Grady knew his father was still in prison, so if you got somethin' to say, please say it, so we can go find our boy."

John remembered the rage he felt when Frank came home from Toppenish and told him what had happened. He remembered the vow he made to himself to end this man's life. Then he remembered Adah's voice: "You can't hate no man forever."

"Yes ma'am. I do got somethin' to say, though. I should have said it a long time ago, I shoulda come to the prison to tell you, but I'm mighty slow at seein' things right sometimes."

He was silent as he looked up and away from the park toward the dark green hills to the east. He paused to let the last twinges of hate, sorrow, and anger subside.

"I know this comes late. But I hold no one responsible for my son's death. I bear you no grudge. Any debt owed, or believed to be owed, I'm forgivin' as of this here instant right now."

Grady Sr. was unable to speak. Beth removed her hand from her husband's arm and reached across the table to place it on John's folded hands.

"Thank you, sir," she said. "We are grateful to you."

"Now then, John said. "There's some things I should tell you about your son. I came down here to find him and a girl he's with. They's both been staying at my place."

"Your place?" Grady Sr. said.

"What girl?" Beth said.

"They was both at my place. They left together 'bout a week ago. I figured Grady'd end up here and we'd find 'im."

Beginning with the rainy afternoon in Ellensburg, John told the story of his time with Grady. He explained that he felt sorry the boy had grown up without his father. He explained that he'd had several opportunities to pick up Grady during the last year, but the time had not seemed right until now. He told about Jill's dead father and Adah's resolute determination that Jill leave with Grady. He smiled when he tried to explain that Adah seemed to know a lot more about Jill and Grady than she should. He said it seemed to Adah that Grady and the girl shared the same missing piece. He told about their son's confrontation with the two boys at the Conoco station and his fight with the boys in Richland.

Beth frowned and shook her head when John talked about the fights. "There were fights in school too," she said, looking into the face of her husband. "He didn't go back after the last one. He said there weren't no use in going back if all he had to do was fight every day. He looked at me and said, 'Mom, I got to fight every day.' I never understood what he meant by that."

Grady Sr. had not moved. "I understand."

The amplified voice of the arena announcer echoed off the empty grandstands. The rodeo would begin soon.

"In the first year after I was locked up, I felt like I'd explode if I didn't get outside the fence. It's like I'd been given a load too heavy to carry, but I couldn't put it down. There was nowhere to drop it. Maybe Grady feels like that."

He paused and looked at his wife. People began moving out of the park and off the street into the arena.

Several quiet moments passed before he spoke again. "Then I met a man who'd already been inside for ten years, and he wasn't getting out any time soon. He's still there. He said he had to let everything go. Just drop it. So, at night I'd stare at the ceilin' and try to remember times with you and times with you and Grady. Times when I rode a good bull. Times even further back when I was a boy."

He paused, continuing to look into his wife's eyes. "Not good times or bad. Just different times goin' on and on, way back."

He stopped again, as if talking at length had become a chore he had forgotten exactly how to do, like walking without a limp. He looked down at his hands folded on the table. He took his right hand and reached across his body to caress his wife's fingers, which were still clutching his forearm. "Then after a while, I come to dream dreams about those times. For the last year or so there was only one dream. I was ridin' a tough bull, but not at a rodeo. In an empty arena. Grady was on the fence, and you was the only one in the stands. I never got bucked off in that dream. Not once."

A loud crashing noise erupted in the arena. John and Grady Sr. looked quickly in that direction. No one at the table said anything. "Mister, I ain't sure what you're doin' here," Grady Sr. said. "My family ain't been together for a good long time now."

Beth watched her husband closely. She put her hands on his hands and said, "I think it might be best if we go on in."

"I understand," John said. "I surely do. Maybe we ought to go on in and see your boy ride that bull.

"Meetin' you was the only thing I feared coming out of jail," Grady Sr. said. "I killed your boy. I swear I didn't mean to. It weren't my intent, but there it is."

Beth nudged closer to her husband. He put his arm around her and continued to speak to John. "There was a time when I wouldn't a' blamed you if you were to want to do the same to me. I feared facin' you. I don't want to cause you no more harm."

"That's not …" John said.

Grady Sr. held up his hand. "I can see now that particular fear don't matter."

John nodded.

Beth sucked in a deep draught of the warm air and shrugged in even closer to her husband and closed her eyes.

"Well then," John said. "Let's go to the rodeo."

CHAPTER 17

Grady hefted his father's old riggin' bag out of the backseat and placed it on the ground. He squatted on his haunches, carefully unzipped the bag, and pulled out his bull rope. The rope had a brass bell attached with a hard knot, placed so it would dangle right beneath the bull's chest.

Next, he unrolled his heavy brown chaps with the black fringe. He shook them out over the top of the bag and carefully checked each of the straps that would wrap loosely around the back of his legs. He checked the buckle that would hold the chaps in place at the small of his back. Some cowboys preferred bright colors—orange and yellow, bright green, even pink. But not Grady. "Keep things simple," his father told him when he was little. "Take what you need and nothing else."

He pulled out his riding glove and checked the seams and the palm for wear. He made sure he had enough white athletic tape to hold the glove in place at the wrist. Finally, he pulled his father's worn glove from the bottom of the bag. It had grown stiff over the years. The palm and the knuckles had worn thin from use then blackened with disuse.

Grady held his right hand in front of his face and carefully pulled on his father's glove. He squeezed it into a fist to stretch the old leather then he opened his hand and spread his fingers. Grady stared into the palm for a long moment. He came out of his crouched position and sat on the ground with his back against John's truck. He placed his gloved hand over his right eye and his bare hand over his left eye. He leaned his head back against the truck and took a deep, slow breath. He exhaled and sat up. After he carefully repacked his gear, he put his riggin' bag over his shoulder and headed for the bucking chutes, his father's worn glove still on his right hand.

He disappeared into the shade behind the chutes beneath the north grandstand and placed his riggin' bag on the ground in front of a bench in a dark corner and sat down. He had inherited his father's obsession with checking and rechecking his riggin' bag. He hated to arrive late to a rodeo because that meant he would have to rush through his routine: Watch the bulls loiter in their pens. Check his draw at the rodeo office. Recheck his riggin' bag. Check the chutes. Test the ground. Find his bull in the pens. Recheck his riggin' bag.

Grady noticed no apparent connection between these habits and a successful ride, but he did not feel ready if he had to rush. When he was much younger, he asked his father why he took more time getting ready than the other bull riders. Grady Sr. told him a cowboy in a hurry might forget something important.

"A bull is a wild, savage thing, so a bull rider can't be reckless," his father said. "You got to control everything you can. Do everything slow. Deliberate. The same way every time. Start movin' too fast and you get ahead of yourself. That's when you get hurt."

Later, long after Grady's father had left, his old bull riding coach, Hazard Quinn, made it clear that being in a hurry meant being careless, and being careless could be fatal.

"A buckin' bull's cold-blooded," Quinn told Grady the day before he rode his first bull. "So, a bull rider can't be. You can't start rushin' around 'cause you're scared. You got to slow down. If you don't, well, that's how a bull rider gets killed."

So, Grady carefully checked each item in his bag again. He kneaded his heavy bull rope inch by inch, paying close attention for any sign of fraying or wear. He made sure the leather grip woven into the rope was sound. Then he returned each item to the bag. The bull rope first this time. Then his tape and rosin can. Then his leather chaps folded neatly and laid flat. He put his long spurs in last, spinning the rowels once and laying them side-by-side on top of his chaps next to his riding gloves. He picked up the bag at each end, hefted it so the contents would settle, and zipped it closed.

He left his riggin' bag on the bench and stepped up onto the wide platform where the cowboys would gather and mingle before climbing over the back of the chutes to settle carefully onto the back of a bucking horse or a bull. He rested his forearms on one of the tall, wooden panels at the back of the chutes and stared out across the green expanse of the infield toward the south grandstand. Grady's bull would be in chute number six. He knew the gate would be in perfect working order, but he climbed down into the chute and swung it open anyway. Then he toed the loose dirt in front of the chute. A good bucking horse will often make his way all the way across Pendleton's grass infield before the eight-second buzzer sounds. At Pendleton it was not uncommon for a riderless bucking horse to find his way onto the half-mile racetrack that encircled the infield and make a panicky dash all the way around the track and the arena before he could be herded into the catch pen.

But a bull seldom got more than twenty or thirty feet outside the chute before the cowboy was bucked off. Even if the animal didn't turn on the grounded cowboy to flip him into the air or grind him into the arena dirt, the bull would take his time and exit precisely when he felt like it, a constant threat, unfazed and unhurried. The cowboy who had just been violently removed from the bull's back was often in considerable discomfort and always in a breathless hurry to escape. As Grady expected the ground in front of the chutes had been carefully groomed. It was level and firm. Following tradition, bull riding was the last event of the day. The ground would harden some, but Grady was satisfied.

Finally, he returned to the pens to watch his bull. He knew what the bull looked like, but he wanted to see how he behaved in the pens. He found the bull and leaned his arms against the steel bar at the top of the pen. The bull stood alone a few feet in front of the other bulls in the same pen. He seemed rooted to the ground with a broad back, short legs, and an enormous head. The bull stared at Grady with empty eyes and did not move. As Grady watched, the bull's entire body began to sway back and forth in perfect time with the rise and fall of his great chest as he breathed. The bull raised his head and locked dull eyes with Grady's own ruthless stare. Soon Grady was breathing in perfect time with the quiet motion of the bull.

"This could be a good'un, big fella," he said.

The bull pawed the ground once with his right front hoof, turned slowly, and walked away.

"This could be a good'un," he said again.

He returned to the area behind the chutes. He sat on the cool ground in front of the bench where he'd placed his riggin' bag and watched the other rough-stock cowboys wander in, usually in pairs or groups of three. It was not uncommon for rough-stock cowboys to travel together. Ropers needed a truck and a trailer to haul their horses and gear and store feed. But a cowboy who rode bucking horses or bulls only needed room for his riggin' bag and maybe a place to stow a bronc saddle. The single trait shared by most young roughies was an ability to sleep anywhere.

Most were louder than Grady when they arrived behind the chutes. Nearly everyone had someone along to help with his bull rope or lend moral support. A few were accompanied by young women, usually in tight Wranglers and new hats, who inevitably hung back unsmiling against the railing at the back of the platform, as far from the bucking chutes as they could get and still be present. Most would be gone by the time the rodeo had begun, sitting together in twos and threes in the grandstand, a mostly silent circle of shared concern.

The boisterous cadre would separate into riders and watchers when the bareback riding began. Anyone not directly involved with horses or cowboys would retreat into the background and the platform would become quiet. Each ride would be followed by a brief blur of questions and commentary when the rider returned to the area behind the chutes. When the last bareback rider returned, assorted injuries would be catalogued and discussed. One or two of the young women would come to the platform, calmer, visibly relieved that the young man they'd come with was unhurt, or at least not badly hurt, and calmly elated if he'd managed a score high enough to warrant a paycheck. Like everyone else associated with the rodeo, they understood the razor-thin margin that separated jackpot from disaster.

The bareback riders would wander away, and the saddle bronc riders would arrive and repeat the process. Through it all, Grady would sit on the ground with his back against the bench, his forearms resting on bent knees. He would not watch the rodeo. He would not greet any of the other cowboys.

As the time to ride his bull drew closer, he would begin to focus more and more intently on an empty spot in the dirt between his feet. He would remain still and quiet until it was time to gear up and warm up for his ride.

✸✸✸

Meanwhile Grady Sr. and Beth found seats in the open east grandstands.

"You don't want to go find Grady, do you?" Beth said. She was nervous.

"Nope. Not now. I know where he is. He's behind the chutes. And I know what he's doin', and I know what he needs to do. He don't need to know we're here. We'll wait. He'll be easy to find later."

✸✸✸

Anne helped Adah navigate her chair through a long row of food venders and souvenir stands to a gate at the southeast end of the rodeo grounds near the ticket booth. They ambled along with the crowd past an enormous, bronze bucking horse. Only the bronc's front feet were on the ground, and the bronze cowboy on his back had his boots eternally buried deep in the stirrups. The rider's old-style, flat-brimmed hat flew away behind him while the cowboy pulled up desperately with one hand on his braided bronc rein. The panicked horse arched his back and ducked his head between his front legs, trying to jerk the rein loose from the cowboy's metallic grip.

Anne stopped and stared up at the statue. "Is that what Grady does?" she said. "Does a bull jump up like that horse?"

"No, darling. Bulls is different," Adah said. "When a bronc bucks a man off, it's natural for him to run away. When a cowboy gets bucked off a bull, the bull usually turns back and comes lookin' for him. The most dangerous part of a bull rider's day is the first few seconds after he hits the ground."

Behind Adah and Anne, Jill froze when she saw her mother. Anne hadn't seen her yet, and Jill didn't quite know what she would to say.

Jill wondered, *what's she doing here*. She knew what most adults would think about her spending a week with Grady. She knew her mother should be furious with her but probably wasn't, and at that moment Jill didn't care much one way or the other.

Since the night her father died, her mother had never, not once, expressed any interest in what Jill was up to. *Maybe because I wasn't up to anything*, Jill thought. She frequently stayed out all night, especially during the warm summer months or anytime it rained, and she once stayed away all weekend. If Anne did ask Jill where she'd been, the girl's petulant "out" and Anne's apathetic "oh" was all there was to the conversation.

Jill didn't have to sneak out. Either she didn't come home from school, or she waited until her mother was asleep and the house was silent before she left. What might have surprised Anne, if her daughter had been inclined to talk about her frequent all-night absences, was the fact that Jill was always alone, walking along the bike path near the river or sitting on a dark park bench watching the deep water drift quietly away.

Jill also knew she hadn't done anything with Grady that would disappoint her father. This was important to her. She wondered if what she had or had not done with Grady mattered to her mother, but since Anne was in Pendleton, Jill realized what she did must matter. She took a deep breath and stepped forward.

"Adah's right," she said. "Grady says bulls are way more dangerous."

Anne spun around at the sound of her daughter's voice. She heard Jill over the murmur of the crowd and the endless chatter of the announcer inside the arena. Jill approached Anne who grabbed her daughter and held her stiffly against her body. She smoothed the girl's brown hair, just as she had when Jill was a child. Jill resisted, but Anne would not release her until the girl pushed her mother gently away.

"Mom, I'm fine."

"Are you? I didn't know where … I don't know what …I guess maybe we should …"

"Talk?" Jill said.

"About that boy?"

"No, mom, not about Grady."

Anne looked relieved. "You're right. Not about Grady."

Anne pulled Jill back toward her and this time the girl did not resist.

"I was scared Jill. For the first time … since … since your father died, I was scared."

"I wasn't scared," Jill said. "For the first time since that night, I wasn't afraid."

Adah cleared her throat and smiled. "Well, that's settled. Let's get goin' before we miss the rodeo. We drove all this way and I want to see what that boy's made of."

Anne laughed uncomfortably, and Jill looked away toward the bucking chutes. Anne pushed Adah's chair through the gate, and Jill turned back and stared at the statue of the horse and bronc rider for another long moment. Then she followed Adah and her mother into the arena.

Once inside, Adah showed Anne how to fold her chair, and Jill carried it up a short set of stairs to their seats about halfway up near the center of the south grandstand, directly across from the bucking chutes. The grandstands were not overly crowded on the first of the rodeo's four days, so they settled in without difficulty.

John arrived a few minutes before the rodeo began. He was surprised to see Jill and whispered to Adah, "When did she show up?"

"I think they've been here all day. No need to talk about it now."

John tipped his hat to Jill, and the girl smiled back.

"How long before Grady?" she asked. "He didn't tell me anything."

"There's a lot more to a rodeo than bull riding," he said. "But most people that ain't ranch people come to see the bulls. It ain't so much that they want to see anyone get hurt, but they don't want to miss a wreck either. There's bareback ridin' and saddle broncs and team ropin' and calf ropin' and steer wrestlin'. Oh, and the girls' barrel racin'. They'll do all that before the bull riders are up."

Jill looked out across Pendleton's grass infield toward dozens of tepees erected just north of the main grandstand. Their seats were directly across from sixteen distinctively colored red, yellow, and blue bucking chutes. John said Grady would be somewhere behind the chutes.

"There are a lot of people here," she said.

"Yes, there is. Pendleton is the biggest rodeo around. There's big shows in Kennewick and Walla Walla. And of course, Ellensburg, but nothin' like Pendleton. You got to go to Cheyenne or Calgary, or maybe the Houston Stock Show to find a bigger show.

"Used to be, folks wouldn't see each other but once a year when they come to town for the round-up. Even now, a lot of these folks'd rather stay at home on the farm or the ranch than come to town regular. When they do come, it's to get feed or do business at the bank, not to visit. The rodeo'll bring 'em in for three or four days in a row. It's always been a big ol' time for ranch folks. Still is."

Suddenly, a cannon shot exploded on the far side of the arena. The rodeo queen and three princesses, all mounted on tall horses, sped into the arena from separate gates at each end of the north grandstand. They raced around the track at a full gallop before sliding to a stop on the grass immediately in front of the south grandstand, directly below where Adah, Anne, Jill, and John sat. Jill was surprised to discover she was thrilled by the galloping horses ridden by young women in flowing green and black chaps and stiff black hats. She grabbed John's arm when one horse nearly went down as a princess raced into the north turn. But the horse collected itself, and the young woman barely moved in the saddle. The horse continued running to the far side of the arena to join the others.

"How about that little lady? Can she sit a horse, or what?" the announcer said, his drawl rising with theatrical excitement.

Jill let go of John's arm. "Is everything that happens down there dangerous?"

"Yeah," he said. "I reckon it is. When you're dealing with livestock, lots can go wrong."

An older cowboy dressed all in black and mounted on a steel-black horse raced into the arena carrying an American flag. Three more young cowgirls followed him, carrying a Canadian flag, an Oregon State Flag, and the banner of the Federated Tribes of the Umatilla Indians. Everyone stood up, Jill more slowly than the rest. A young Indian girl sang the "Star-Spangled Banner."

"Are there any proud Americans here this afternoon?" the announcer asked. The crowd cheered with a single voice. "Then let's get ready to rodeooooo!" Rock music replaced the announcer's voice, and everyone sat down.

"The bareback riding is first," John said. Across the arena the first bucking horse was already out of the chute. The thin young man on his back raked the horse's shoulders with his spurs in perfect rhythm with horse's violent bucking motion. The eight-second buzzer sounded and two tall cowboys riding very tall horses galloped in to help the rider dismount. There were fourteen bareback riders.

Jill sat through the calf roping and steer wrestling. The speed and power of the horses excited her. The skill of the cowboys, even though she had no idea what the object was in any of the events, impressed her. The horses and most of the cowboys seemed to know what they were doing. John tried to explain each event as it came up, and she tried to listen. But things happened so fast she didn't have time to absorb much of his explanations.

Next came the saddle bronc riders. John explained that this event was probably the most like bull riding because the cowboy had to sit up tall and balance against a braided bronc rein attached to a heavy halter. Jill noticed that fewer of these cowboys stayed on than in the bareback event. Next came team roping, the event that confused Jill the most.

"You got one cowboy that's going to come out on the left and rope the steer's horns," John said. "Then when his horse turns the steer to the left, his partner's goin' to come up and rope both back legs. Then the horses will turn to face each other and stretch the steer. It's a tough event because there's five brains, and they all got to be thinkin' in the same direction."

"Doesn't it hurt?"

"Well, sometimes a cowboy will catch his thumb in the dally, or the end of the rope might come loose and snap the cowboy on the hand, but mostly I don't think…"

"No. Doesn't it hurt the cow?"

"It's a steer, honey. And I don't reckon it bothers them much. They're all goin' to be hamburger anyway."

His remark almost made her smile, but then she remembered all the fast food she'd eaten and turned up her nose.

"Just one more event to go then the bull riders'll be up," he said.

A new pickup came into the arena and three men set up three fifty-five-gallon barrels in a triangle pattern.

"The barrel racin' at Pendleton's little different than at most rodeos," he said. "Most of the arena here is taken up by the grass infield of the racetrack, so they set the barrels up on the track. It makes the race about twice as long as usual. A girl's got to have a horse that can really run to win here. Some ol' boys don't like the barrel racin', but I can't think a too many things prettier than a horse runnin' full out. And they got to run full out here."

Just as he finished speaking, the first rider rode across the grass from the west end of the arena. Her horse ran hard to the first barrel, and Jill was certain the horse was going to run all the way into the first row of the grandstand. At the last instant, the horse dropped his back end hard, slid just past the barrel and then snapped back to the right and on across the grass infield toward the north grandstand and the second barrel. The horse and rider turned back to the left this time and galloped away to the third barrel. After another hard left turn, the horse and rider raced all the way back toward the west end of the arena where they'd begun. Twelve girls raced around the barrels. Jill was thrilled with each run. Two girls knocked a barrel over. "They'll add five seconds to their time when that happens," John explained. A lull occurred while the new pickup returned to remove the barrels.

"Well, what you think of the rodeo so far?" he asked.

"I'm not sure what's going, but it's sort of exciting, or scary anyway."

"Yeah. It is. I suppose it's hard to stay numb at the rodeo. You get to wonderin' what's goin' to happen to those young folks in the arena, hopin' no one gets hurt. A lotta folks come and forget their own troubles for a time. Crops might be bad or cattle prices low. Rain might not a come when you need it. The bank may be makin' threats. Your kids might be takin' up with the wrong sort. All that gets forgotten for a little while at the rodeo."

Jill looked away, recalling for the first time the details of the wreck. "I haven't forgotten anything … Daddy, I remember."

John heard her but did not say anything.

The loud rock music began again. The announcer shouted, "Are you ready for some bull ridin'?" The crowd cheered louder than at any other time all day.

Anne leaned across Adah's lap. The speed and the uncertainty of each rodeo event terrified her. "Jill, honey. Are you going to be okay?"

"Mom, please don't." Anne sat back and was silent.

The first bull sprang out of the chute and a stocky cowboy was bucked off almost immediately. The next four met a similar fate. The sixth bull rider nearly made it to the eight-second buzzer, but he was bucked off hard and was dazed after he hit the ground headfirst. He tried to get up, but just as he reached his hands and knees, the bull turned on him, got both horns under his chest, and threw him about six feet in the air. On the way down, he crashed into the chute, bounced off the wooden gate, hit the ground hard again, and did not move.

The two bullfighters finally got the bull distracted. The bull stared at the nearest bullfighter for a moment and then jogged nonchalantly out of the arena. Jill was on her feet with the knuckles of both hands pressed against her mouth. She stared at the cowboy lying still on the ground and then scanned the bucking chutes for Grady. He was standing in chute number six, straddling his bull and paying no attention to the cowboy who'd been hurt.

"Look," John said. "That boy's tryin' to sit up. He'll be okay I 'spect."

Jill took a quick glance in the direction of the fallen cowboy. Two older men were helping him sit up. He rolled his head back and leaned back weakly against the same chute gate he'd crashed into when the bull flung him in the air. Soon an ambulance entered the arena and paramedics were hovering over the injured cowboy. He tried to get up on his own, but as soon as he tried to stand, his knees buckled and the two older men, one on each arm, supported him as he folded slowly and unconsciously onto the ground. The paramedics, several other bull riders, and the rodeo clowns carefully loaded the cowboy onto a stretcher and lifted him into the ambulance. With no lights flashing, the ambulance drove out of the arena.

"Ain't a rodeo fun?" Adah said. "Bull riders is mostly fools."

Jill was still standing, and she had begun to tremble. To steady herself, she put her hand on John's arm again. They sat down, and he patted the girl's hand. "It's all going to be okay. You'll see."

Finally, the judges called Grady's name. He knew a boy had been hurt, but he didn't know how badly, and he would not allow himself to be concerned. He did not think about the ambulance that had just left the arena. No one else had stayed on yet, so he knew he would win a check if he could ride the bull named Freeway, even if the last four cowboys, all more experienced than Grady, managed to ride for the full eight seconds.

The rodeo announcer was telling the crowd about Grady, "Next up is a young cowboy from up north across the river. He's won a little bit a' money this summer, and he's come to Pendleton to take on the big boys. He came within about a half second a' winning the Ellensburg Bull-o-Rama and you can bet he'll be tryin' even harder for you folks today. Hazard Quinn taught him to ride bulls real good. From Richland, Washington, Grady Cross on Freeway. There been some good scores on this old bull. But a' course, you got to stay on to get paid. Get a good seat, Grady. Hang on, son!"

Jill barely heard the announcer as he continued to tell the crowd about the bull and a little more about Grady. Her attention was focused on the cowboy across the arena in chute number six. She could see Grady standing above the bull, but she could not tell what was going on inside the chute.

Grady had climbed into the chute and straddled the bull with one foot on the rails of the gate and the other on the wooden panel at the back of the chute. A large cowboy, much older than Grady, was trying to get Grady's bull rope around the bull with a long wire hook. Finally, he pulled the rope up around the bull's chest, just behind his front legs. Grady thanked him and pulled the long, loose end of the rope through a loop braided into the other end. He pulled the rope snug and carefully sat down on the bull's broad back. The older cowboy pulled the loose end of the bull rope tight, and the bull leaned forward. Grady took the loose end from the older man and pulled it tighter yet. The bull leaned back against the back end of the chute. Grady knew the monster was preparing for the two explosive jumps he expected as soon as the gate opened.

He slid his right hand, palm up, into the leather handle and ran the loose end of the rope across his palm. He squeezed his fist closed then pounded his fingers down with his left fist. He flipped the loose end of the rope across the bull to the right and settled down slowly. He dropped his feet to each side of the bull and squeezed gently, nudging the long spurs on the heels of his boots slowly into the bull's side. The bull leaned back even harder. Grady pulled up on the rope with his right hand and pushed his hips forward. He nodded, and the gate swung open.

In the grandstand, Jill gasped when the bull roared out of the chute and took two enormous jumps across the narrow racetrack toward the grass infield. Grady nearly lost his seat when the bull stumbled to the right on the first jump. He dug the spur on his left foot into the bull's side and pulled up harder on the rope with his right hand. He was well-centered on the second jump, in a favorable position when the bull began to spin into his right hand. The bull's head was twisted far around to the right as he tried to dig his single, short horn into Grady's leg. He nearly came off on the second spin, but he locked himself in with his left foot and hung on. Grady felt his hand begin to slide away from the bull rope, and he squeezed as hard as he could with both legs and tried to draw the tips of his fingers down through the palm of his clenched fist. He kept his chin down and focused all his strength on keeping his fingers wrapped around the bull rope.

Grady thought he heard the eight-second buzzer, but he wasn't certain, so he stayed with the bull for one more spin before giving up his grip. The bull stopped abruptly as Grady pulled his hand out of the rope, threw his left leg over the bull's head, and slid to the ground, landing upright on both feet. He glanced back over his shoulder to see the bull begin to turn in his direction. The bullfighters were already racing in front of the bull, and Grady was able to jog back toward the chute.

He stopped to face the grandstand and was aware for the first time that the crowd was on its feet. He threw his hat high in the air toward the crowd in the main grandstand, just as one of the bullfighters returned his bull rope and just as the announcer said, "We have the first qualified ride of the Pendleton Round-Up, and it's a goodun! Eight-five points for the up-and-coming kid from

Richland, Washington. That boy'll be buying dinner for someone tonight."

Grady felt weak in the knees. He returned to chute number six, climbed over the back, and sat down hard on a bench bolted to the wide, wooden platform. Other cowboys and several chute workers came by to offer congratulatory handshakes and pats on the back. Grady had begun to remove the athletic tape that held his riding glove in place when he noticed for the first time that he was still wearing his father's old glove.

The last two bull riders both stayed on, but neither scored more than eighty points.

***

"Come on," John said. "We got to meet some people before we find Grady."

"What people?" Jill said.

"Jill, it may not be any of your business," Anne said.

"Then why'd he say *we* had to meet some people? Is it Frank?"

"Frank'll be at the truck when it's time to go," Adah said. "I'm sure he found something to do behind the chutes."

John picked up the folded wheelchair and then helped Adah to her feet. People around them politely moved aside when they saw that Adah needed help. She leaned on John's arm as they made their way carefully down the stairs. At the bottom, John asked her if she wanted to walk.

"I think I can make it for a while," she said. They drifted along with the crowd until they exited the arena past the statue. The bronze cowboy still had not been bucked off. Standing just outside the gate and a little to the left were Grady's parents.

"These folks are Grady's momma and daddy," John said. "And this is Anne and her girl, Jill. I told you about Jill."

"Yes, Jill," Beth said. "John says you know our Grady."

"A little," she said, and her cheeks reddened.

Anne coughed and turned away.

"Well, isn't this nice?" Adah said sweetly. The presence of Grady's mother and father had caused her to perk up. "I'm so glad everyone is here. I do hope there ain't goin' to be any trouble." She gave John a hard look.

Beth took Adah's hand. Her husband stayed back until Beth turned and nodded toward Adah.

"I'm pleased to meet you, ma'am," he said.

"Well, you got better manners than most jailbirds," Adah said. Anne was appalled, but Grady Sr. laughed.

"We're goin' to get along fine," John said. "We talked already. But right now, we got to find that boy."

Grady sat behind the chutes accepting congratulations. Not only had he won a big check, but he would also be back on Saturday for the short go with a chance to win again. He repacked his riggin' bag, but he placed his father's glove in his back pocket, the fingers dangling out behind him, and went to find Jill. He did not have to go far. Everyone was waiting for Grady just outside the fence near the stock pens, John and Adah in front with Jill and her mother standing back. Grady did not immediately notice his own mother and father waiting back and to one side. Grady Sr. leaned heavily on his walking stick.

"That was a nice ride," John said.

"What happened to the boy who got hurt?" Jill asked.

The question surprised Grady. He stared at Jill for a moment, angry that she would ask about the injured cowboy before she said anything about his ride. "I don't know. I guess they took him to the hospital. He must not a' died or we woulda heard."

He swung his riggin' bag over his shoulder and started off toward the rodeo office.

"Grady," Beth said. "Son, your father is here."

The sound of his mother's voice surprised him. He stopped and turned back. His father took a step forward.

"That was a good ride, son. Made me proud."

Grady was stunned. He shrugged the riggin' bag off his shoulder and let it slide to the ground, the strap dangling loosely in his right hand. After a moment he hefted the bag onto his shoulder and started to walk away. He stopped again and turned halfway back toward where his father was standing.

"I got to pick up my check." He looked at his father and thought of the long years he'd been gone. Then, with his father suddenly present and standing there before him, the memory of those years faded until it seemed Grady Sr. had never been gone at all.

"It's been a long time, son," Grady Sr. said. "I know it's been a long time."

"Not so long," Grady said. "I'm goin' to get paid. You want to come along?"

Grady Sr. handed his walking stick to Beth. He pulled himself erect and walked with little pain to his son. He put his hand on Grady's shoulder and father and son headed for the rodeo office. The fingers of his father's old, worn riding glove still dangled out of Grady's back pocket.

CHAPTER 18

"Well," Beth said. "What now?"

"Was that really Grady's dad?" Jill said.

"Jill!" Anne said. "It's not our business."

"The *hell* it *ain't*," Jill said, knowing her mother did not appreciate profanity or lax grammar. Anne sighed and shook her head.

"I'll just go find Frank and have 'im bring his truck around here," John said. He could see Jill was agitated, wanting to know more about Grady's father. "Want to come along, Jill, or stay here with the women?"

John started off. Jill looked at her mother and decided that staying would not get her any closer to finding out about Grady's father. "I'm coming with you. Wait up."

Anne took Jill by the arm. "Jill, stay here!"

Adah tapped Anne on the shoulder and nodded toward a bench next to the small warm-up arena. Anne released her daughter and helped Adah to the bench and sat down next to her. Beth watched her husband and son walk away and then introduced herself to Anne. Adah smiled and patted the bench to indicate that Beth should sit down.

"Let's get acquainted," Adah said.

Jill rolled her eyes and started after John. Anne started to get up to follow, but Adah grasped her arm just above the wrist and pulled her back down.

***

Frank watched Grady's ride from the area near the roping chute at the west end of the arena. When the bull riding ended, Frank correctly guessed John and the rest would meet Grady somewhere behind the main grandstand. He waited until the crowd thinned out then headed that way. As he came around the far end of the warm-up arena, he spotted Grady walking back toward the rodeo office with a man he knew all too well.

What's he doin' here? Did John and Adah know he'd be here? I don't want nothin' to do with that man.

Frank turned away from the reunion and headed back toward his truck, still parked on the street across from the park. When he reached the truck, he got in and sat behind the wheel for a long time and thought about what to do next.

I could go back there and beat the tar out of him. He looked a might stove up. Or I could kill 'im. Frank reached under the seat and pulled out a heavy old-style revolver and set it on the seat next to him.

John and Jill had cut through the Indian village. They finally emerged from the rodeo grounds and crossed the park. As they approached the truck, they could see Frank sitting behind the wheel.

"Good," John said. "We won't have to hunt 'im down."

Just as John finished talking, Frank started the truck and did a clumsy U-turn and headed back toward the area behind the main grandstand where he'd seen Grady and his father. John waved at his son, but Frank either did not see John and Jill or he ignored them.

"Is he leaving without us?" Jill said. "That can't be good."

"Come on, girl. We got to get back to Adah."

Frank worked his way impatiently through the slow-moving traffic about three blocks along Court St. until he reached the wide gate at the competitors' entrance. He jammed his truck into a hard right turn and stopped.

"I just need to pick up my brother back here," he told the guard at the gate. "He was banged up in the bull ridin'."

"Rodeo's over for today," the guard said. "Come ahead."

Frank nodded at the guard and made his way slowly along the gravel road in front of the rodeo office. He saw Grady and his father heading back in the direction they'd come. Grady was folding his check in half and slipping it carefully into his shirt pocket. Frank slowed the truck and followed at a discreet distance. As Grady and his father approached the bench where Adah was sitting, Frank pulled his truck into a spot that had just been vacated by a rig leaving the rodeo grounds. He watched Grady and his father in the rearview mirror until they reached the bench, then he got out of the truck and started walking slowly toward the inevitable confrontation he'd anticipated and feared for more than six years.

***

Success in the rodeo world never had much to do with appearances. Rodeo success was a matter of simple arithmetic, determined by whether a cowboy ended up on the plus or minus side of an equation with expenses paid out on one side and cash won on the other. No one got paid for showing up. Either you rode your bull better than the other guys, or you roped your calf faster than the other guys. How good you were in the last rodeo didn't matter. How much money you won today was all that counted.

Since Grady understood this fundamental aspect of rodeo, he also understood why the first thing his father said when he came out of the rodeo office with his check was, "How much did you win?"

"Four thousand, six hundred, and twenty-eight dollars," Grady said. He held up the check and waved it like a flag. As he and Grady Sr. began to walk back toward the bench where they'd left Adah, Beth, and Anne, he folded the check in half and put it in the pocket of his shirt. Neither Grady nor his father was aware that Frank had been following them slowly in his truck.

Frank parked and got out of his truck just as John and Jill emerged from the Indian village. Anne got up when she saw them.

"They're back," she said.

Adah turned to see Grady and his father approaching, and she saw Frank following on foot. He stopped about thirty feet from the others. Adah motioned for Beth and Anne to help her stand.

CHAPTER 19

"Well, you're finally here," Adah said. "Frank, son, come on over and join us. Some things goin' to get said. I wasn't sure you'd want to be here."

"I'll stay back here. See what I can see," Frank said.

There were still people milling around after the rodeo. But family groups gathering to meet contestants were not uncommon, so no one took any particular notice.

"Come here," Adah said. "Folk's goin' to start starin'."

"What's all this about?" Jill said. "Adah, what's going on?"

Frank was staring at Jill. She held Frank's eyes for a few seconds before brushing past. Anne came forward and stood with her daughter.

"Mom, what's going on?"

Anne shook her head and shrugged. The sound of horses galloping in the arena diverted Jill's attention. Frank had moved in closer. "What's he doin' here?" he said, motioning toward Grady Sr. with his chin. "Ain't he 'sposed to be in jail still?"

Grady Sr. moved an awkward step or two away from the others. Beth took his arm, but he slowly pulled away. "What do you want from me? I didn't intend for your brother to die."

"But he did," Frank said. He slowly reached under his shirt and pulled the .45 out of his belt and let the gun hang down at his side.

"Frank!" John said. "Put that away, son. There's no need for that."

"There is a need for this gun. Yessir." He raised the pistol to his temple. "Yessir."

Anne was horrified. She put her arm around Jill's shoulder. Jill looked at her mother and whispered at Grady Sr., "What were you in prison for?"

"I killed John's son."

Then, haunted, as he'd been every day for more than six years, Frank sobbed once and cocked the revolver.

✳✳✳

Grady Sr. stepped away from his young wife and looked once more at the boy sleeping on the couch before climbing behind the wheel of his pickup and driving away from their small house for the last time.

He traveled first to Baker, Oregon, where he won enough money to get to California and to send $500 home. In Weed he was bucked off. In Fresno he drew an easy bull but won only enough money to get to Bakersfield, where he won another check, and again, sent money home. He drew big in Fallon, Nevada but was bucked off. After two more fruitless rodeos in Oregon, he headed home with just one more stop to make and one more bull to ride.

Toppenish, Washington was the geographical and cultural axis of the Yakima Valley. The home of the Yakama Nation Cultural Center, it was surrounded by orchards, vineyards, dairy farms, cattle ranches, and the world's largest hop field. The population of the surrounding countryside was roughly one-third anglo, one-third Hispanic, and one-third American Indian.

Before his last ride, Grady Sr. stood above the chute in Toppenish the way he always did. He leaned lightly on the top rail at the back of the chute and watched the bull rock nervously back and forth. Two other bull riders were up before Grady Sr. Both were bucked off. The second was gored in the thigh when he was unable to roll out of the bull's way. He hopped back to the chute after the bullfighters finally got the bull distracted. The announcer was saying something about how the cowboy would be okay as soon as the paramedics got a look at him. Then the announcer said something about the next cowboy being from just up the road in Benton City. He was vaguely aware of the crowd's polite applause, but when the judges called for him to get on his bull, his mind went blank.

When his bull rope had been secured around the bull's deep chest, he dropped into a squatting position and leaned back to stretch the hard muscles in his thighs and lower back. Then he climbed carefully over the top rail and settled gently onto the back of the bull. The bull arched his back, and the enormous hump behind his head began to quiver as soon as Grady Sr. sat down.

Another cowboy pulled the loose end of the rope tight. Grady Sr. ran his gloved right hand up and down the rope several times to heat the rosin, so the rope would not slip when the bull jumped out of the chute. He slipped his right hand into the leather grip woven into the rope. The cowboy pulled the loose end up hard and the rope tightened around the bull's chest.

The bull leaned back suddenly and lunged forward, but Grady Sr. had placed his feet lightly on the steel supports on each side of the chute, so he could stand up a couple of inches to let the bull relax. He took the loose end of the rope from the cowboy and pulled it down tightly against his open right hand. He pounded the fingers of his right hand shut with his left fist and flipped the remainder of the loose end of the rope to the right side of the bull. Finally, he pulled his black hat down as tightly as he could, dropped his chin, and nodded.

The gate man hesitated for a second then the gate that formed the left side of the bucking chute swung open. The bull lunged sideways and jumped straight up in the air three times. On the first jump, Grady Sr. thought, *this will be a big score.* Then, without warning, the bull began to spin back to the left, away from the rider's right-handed grip. Surprised, Grady Sr. shifted his weight slightly to counteract the centrifugal force generated by the spinning bull. As he reeled, the bull raised its head, trying to gouge his leg with the tip of its left horn.

He hooked the bull with his left spur and kicked it hard three or four times on the right side. The bull continued to spin, and he felt his hand coming loose. He stopped spurring and focused all the strength he could muster on squeezing his legs and maintaining his handhold. His hand came loose, and the buzzer sounded. He came off the back of the bull, was flung high in the air by the huge animal's last jump, flipped once, and landed on his hands and knees. The bull turned back on him, but one of the bullfighters, the red, white, and blue streamers from his clown costume distracting the bull, dashed between Grady Sr. and the animal. The bull turned his attention to the bullfighter, who sprinted off to the right and into the exit gate. The bull followed slowly.

Grady Sr. heard the cheers of the crowd. "Did he make it?!" the announcer screamed. "He's got a thumbs-up from the judges. Here's the score. Eighty-nine points! The man from up the road will take the lead in the go-round and he could win the whole shootin' match."

He took off his hat and flung it toward the crowd. The hat rose in the air then returned like a boomerang. He picked it up and took his bull rope from the other bullfighter as he jogged off toward the chutes. The gate was still open, so he climbed up the backside of the chute and accepted congratulations from the other bull riders. He watched the last two riders in the rodeo try to match his score, but both cowboys were bucked off early. Grady's father had won. He packed his gear neatly in his riggin' bag, found a pay phone, called his wife, and spoke briefly with Grady, who was excited to learn his father hadn't been bucked off. Since Toppenish was only an hour from Benton City, he'd be home later that night with a big check.

Then he took a shower in the crude restroom next to the pens where the bulls and bucking horses lounged before being loaded into huge stock trucks for the journey home or to the next rodeo. He dressed in the same dusty jeans and a clean shirt, hefted his riggin' bag onto his shoulder, and went to the rodeo office to pick up his check. He folded the check in half, put it in the pocket of his clean shirt, and headed to his truck for the drive home.

In the grass parking lot behind the rodeo arena, Grady Sr. came upon a small gathering of young cowboys who were celebrating loudly and drinking beer from a cooler in the bed of a pickup truck. As he made his way past the rowdy cowboys, a short, stocky young man in a beat-up hat, staggered a few feet away from the noisy circle and grabbed Grady Sr. by the arm.

"Hey, I know you," he said. "This here hotshot won the bull riding tonight," he said to his friends. His voice was slurred, and he was waving his beer can in the direction of Grady Sr. "Hey hotshot, have a beer with us. You weren't the only winner from Benton City tonight. I won the calf ropin'. Bet you didn't know there was another ro-de-o champeen from Benton City. It's a big night for our little town. Have a beer with us, hotshot."

"No thanks. I got to get on home. I've been on the road for a few weeks now."

"Well, you can just get right on home after you have a beer with us. Come on, dude, the rodeo's over. You can take a minute to have a beer."

"No, I gotta go." He began to walk away.

"No, you don't got to go."

The cowboy threw his beer down. Warm foam fizzed out of the overturned can. The cowboy grabbed Grady Sr.'s right shoulder with his left hand. He spun the older man around and hit him hard with his right fist. The blow staggered Grady Sr., but he did not go down. He regained his balance and took a menacing step toward the cowboy. The cowboy swung again, but this time Grady Sr. leaned away from the wild punch. The force of the missed punch swung the cowboy around. Grady Sr. grabbed the cowboy by the shirt near the shoulders and slammed his head into the tailgate of the pickup truck. The cowboy went rigid for an instant then slumped to the ground.

Grady Sr. stood over the young man for a few seconds then turned to walk away, but this time, five of the six cowboys who had been drinking with the unconscious young man surrounded him. Only Frank stayed back.

"You ain't goin' nowhere," one of the cowboys said.

Frank stepped into the group and gently pushed the ringleader away. "Let him go," he said. "Charlie started it. He's just got a bump on the head. Let the man go on home." Grady Sr. pushed his way out of the circle and disappeared into dark parking lot.

"You gonna take care of your brother, Frank?" the cowboy who had spoken before asked.

"Yeah. I'll get him home."

"Fine. Let's go get some more beer, boys." They left Frank alone to take care of Charlie. Frank's brother had fallen to the ground face down and was snoring loudly. He knelt beside the younger man, turned him over, and shook him awake.

"You okay, Charlie?"

He helped him sit up. There was no blood showing. Charlie shook his head and said, "Help me up, brother. I'm gonna git 'im good."

He helped his brother to his feet and said, "It's over. You had no call to do him that way. The man just wanted to go home."

"It ain't over 'til I get my licks in. Where'd he go? The bull riders mostly park back along the fence so they can sleep in their rigs." He started off in that direction.

"No," Frank said. "You ain't going to fight him no more. Come on. We're goin' home."

Charlie tried to push past Frank, but Frank was too strong, and his brother was still unsteady. Frank grabbed him by the collar and shoved him hard back toward the pickup. The cowboy's boots slipped on the grass, and he fell awkwardly. His head made a sickening thud as it hit the rigid steel bumper of the truck, and he went limp. Charlie's body plopped to the ground and did not move.

✳✳✳

"He didn't do it!" Frank screamed. People who had been milling around after the rodeo heard Frank, saw the gun, and began to scatter. He looked at his father. "*I* did it. It was an accident, but I did it."

Grady Sr. did not move. Beth grabbed his left arm with both hands. He gently pried first one hand away, then the other. He placed a hand on her shoulder and slowly nudged her behind him. Frank had dropped to his knees, the gun still pressed against his temple. "Yes, sir. It's been Hell, but I got nowhere else to go." He looked up at John, pleading. "It was *me*."

Grady Sr. took four very quick, painful steps toward Frank. He grabbed his right wrist just as Frank pulled the trigger. The explosive report of the big handgun panicked the few bystanders who had stayed close enough to watch. Anne screamed. Beth called her husband's name. John pulled Adah to him and put his body between her and Frank. Jill did not move. Grady had begun to shake.

Grady Sr. had jerked Frank's gun hand down. The heavy bullet had torn a hole in Frank's jeans and passed through the big muscle on the inside of Frank's leg before burying itself in the ground. John stepped away from Adah and moved toward his son. Grady Sr. took the gun from Frank and handed it to John.

"John looked up at Grady Sr. "Thank you for my boy," he said.

John tried to help Frank to his feet. But there was no fight left, and Frank remained on his knees. A crimson circle spread out rapidly on the leg of his jeans, and blood began to drip onto the ground.

A police car with its lights flashing entered through the competitors' entrance. John and Grady Sr. looked around. Everyone appeared to have frozen in place.

Except Grady.

"You are a deadman!" he screamed. Grady rushed Frank, but Jill stepped in front of him and planted both hands in the center of his chest and grabbed his shirt. Surprised by the force in Jill's slight body, Grady stopped in his tracks.

"Why do this? It's over."

"No!" He grabbed Jill by both wrists and started to fling her aside.

"Grady!" Adah said. "Don't do it, boy."

Grady stopped and stared first at Adah and then back at Jill, who had not moved and who had not taken her eyes off Grady's face. She was breathing hard, and Grady released her wrists. Jill stepped in closer. Grady watched Frank who was still on the ground. John was supporting him with arm around Frank's shoulders while one policeman worked at getting the bleeding to stop and the other took possession of Frank's gun. The paramedics from the ambulance, which was parked near the rodeo office, approached cautiously on foot. Bystanders and onlookers had begun to reassemble. Grady Sr. had stepped back away from Frank and John, and Beth had moved up next to her husband. She tried to give the walking stick to Grady Sr., but he shook his head and watched Grady and Jill.

Grady relaxed his shoulders and turned back to Jill. He stared at her and was startled by something fierce and in the girl's eyes, some strength welling up from deep inside. He stepped back and wondered why no one had ever stopped him from fighting before.

Jill reached up and put one hand on each side of Grady's face. "There's no need. *Your* father is back." And Grady felt the persistent anger harden into an unfamiliar shame. He stepped away. Jill took his hand and led him to his parents, then returned to her mother.

"Did you know that if Daddy hadn't pushed me out of the car, we both would have died?"

Anne shook her head. She covered her face with both hands and sobbed silently. Jill put both arms around her mother and held her while she cried.

"Glory be," Adah said. "Thank you, Jesus."

About the Author

Bruce Blizard is a former journalist, teacher and coach in Washington State. He lives on 25 acres with Tina, his wife of 46 years, and various dogs, cats, and horses. *God's Instant* is his first book. In addition to *God's Instant, A Better Place, and Always a Runner.* His fourth book *The Right Kind of Boy* will be released in August of 2021.